American
Fairy Tales

American Fairy Tales

From Rip Van Winkle to the Rootabaga Stories

Compiled by Neil Philip

Illustrated by Michael McCurdy

Preface by Alison Lurie

HYPERION
NEW YORK

For Mary-Elizabeth and Patrick — N. P.

Conceived, designed, and produced by The Albion Press Ltd.,
Spring Hill, Idbury, Oxfordshire OX7 6RU, United Kingdom.

Volume © 1996 by The Albion Press Ltd.
Selection, story prefaces, and afterword © 1996 by Neil Philip.
Illustrations © 1996 by Michael McCurdy.
Preface © 1996 by Alison Lurie.

"How They Broke Away to Go to the Rootabaga Country" from *Rootabaga Stories* by
Carl Sandburg, © 1922, 1923 by Harcourt, Brace and Company, and renewed 1950,
1951 by Carl Sandburg, reprinted by permission of the publisher.

Printed in Hong Kong.

First Edition

3 5 7 9 10 8 6 4 2

Library of Congress Cataloging-in-Publication Data

American fairy tales / selected by Neil Philip ; illustrated by
Michael McCurdy. — 1st U.S. ed.
    p.   cm.
    Summary: Includes works and discussion of Washington Irving,
Horace E. Scudder, M. S. B., Frank Stockton, Howard Pyle, Louisa May
Alcott, L. Frank Baum, Laura E. Richards, Ruth Plumly Thompson, Will
Bradley, Carl Sandburg, and Neil Philip.
    ISBN 0-7868-0207-3 (trade) — ISBN 0-7868-2171-X (lib. bdg.)
    1. Fairy tales–United States.   2. Children's stories, American.
[1. Fairy tales.   2. Short stories.]   I. Philip, Neil.
II. McCurdy, Michael, ill.
IN PROCESS
[Fic]—dc20   95-49143

This book is set in 14 on 17 point Perpetua.
Designed by Emma Bradford.
Typesetting by York House Typographic Ltd., London, U.K.

CONTENTS

PREFACE

The idea of an "American fairy tale" may arouse disbelief. Fairy tales, for most of us, are the European ones we read as children, the same ones that our children are reading now: "Snow White," "Cinderella," "Beauty and the Beast," "Jack and the Beanstalk." In the last century it was even suggested that America didn't need fairy tales. Instead of imaginary wonders we had the natural wonders of a new continent: Indians and wild animals instead of sprites and dragons; Niagara Falls and the Rockies instead of enchanted lakes and mountains.

However, Americans *were* writing fairy tales — though, like the European ones, they seldom contained actual fairies. Sometimes these tales featured old fashioned props and characters: magic potions and spells, dwarves and witches, princes and princesses. But often they also included contemporary objects and figures: hotels and telephones, mayors and gold miners. And even from the beginning many of the best American stories had a different underlying message than the ones from across the Atlantic.

The standard European fairy tale takes place in a fixed social world. In the usual plot a poor boy or girl, through some combination of luck, courage, beauty, kindness, and supernatural help, becomes rich or marries into royalty. In a variation, a prince or princess who has fallen under an evil enchantment, or been cast out by a cruel relative, regains his or her rightful position. In both types of story the social system is unquestioned and remains unchanged. What the characters hope for is to succeed within the terms of this system.

What makes American fairy tales unique is that in the most interesting of them this does not happen. Instead, the world within the story alters or is abandoned. Rip Van Winkle falls into a twenty-year sleep and wakes to find that a British colony has become a new nation in which "the very character of the people seemed changed." A hundred years later, the family in Carl Sandburg's story repeats the experience of many nineteenth-century immigrants and Western settlers. They sell all their possessions and ride to "where the railroad tracks run off into the sky" — to Rootabaga Country, which is not a fairy kingdom but rich farming country named after a large turnip.

In American fairy tales, even if the world does not change, its values are often implicitly criticized. The traditional European tales, though full of wicked step-mothers and cruel kings and queens, seldom attack the institutions of marriage or monarchy. They assume that what the heroine or hero wants is to become rich and marry well — if possible, into royalty.

Although a few American tales follow this convention, many do not. The guests who visit "The Rich Man's Place," in Horace Scudder's story, enjoy the palatial house and grounds but don't express a desire to live there. In Frank Stockton's "The Bee-man of Orn," a Junior Sorcerer discovers that an old beekeeper has been "transformed" from his original shape, and sets out to dissolve the enchant-ment. But as it turns out, the Bee-man's original shape (like everyone's) was that of a baby. Although the Junior Sorcerer restores him to infancy, when he grows up he does not become a prince, but a beekeeper again — and, as before, he is perfectly contented.

In American fairy tales, there is often not much to be said for wealth and high position, or even good looks. The witch in Hawthorne's "Feathertop" turns a scarecrow into a fine gentleman and sends him out into the world, where he exposes the superficiality and snobbery of the well-to-do. In L. Frank Baum's "The Glass Dog," the poor glass-blower manages to marry a princess, but she "was very jealous of his beauty and led him a dog's life."

The implication of such stories is that an American does not need to become rich or "marry up" in order to be happy; in fact, one should avoid doing so if pos-sible. Happiness is all around one already, as the boy in Laura Richards's "The Golden Windows" discovers: his farmhouse already has "windows of gold and dia-mond" when the setting sun shines on it. Today, when there is so much pressure on Americans to want fame, power, and expensive objects, to feel dissatisfied with themselves and their possessions, these American fairy tales still have some-thing to tell us.

— Alison Lurie

Professor of American Literature, Cornell University

RIP VAN WINKLE

———◆◆◆◆———

WASHINGTON IRVING

Washington Irving (1783–1859) was born in New York City. After training as a lawyer, he turned to writing, making his name as an author with **The Sketch Book of Geoffrey Crayon, Gent.** *(1819–20), a miscellany of essays and stories that contained both "Rip Van Winkle" and "The Legend of Sleepy Hollow." These were the first serious attempts to relocate European folktales in America. Though Irving could have found similar ideas in Native American tales, or in many other cultures, "Rip Van Winkle" was in fact suggested by the German legend of the Emperor Barbarossa's long sleep in the Kyffhäuser mountains. But Irving insisted that the pseudonymous "Diedrich Knickerbocker" was the story's true author, and that its origins and contents were entirely American and wholly verifiable as fact. He claimed Knickerbocker had spoken to Rip Van Winkle himself, and also "seen a certificate on the subject, taken before a country justice, and signed with a cross, in the justice's own handwriting. The story, therefore, is beyond the possibility of doubt." Just such irrefutable "evidence" is often used to justify the American tall tale. However, for the purposes of this book the framing material by "Crayon" and "Knickerbocker" has been omitted.*

WHOEVER HAS made a voyage up the Hudson must remember the Kaatskill mountains. They are a dismembered branch of the great Appalachian family, and are seen away to the west of the river, swelling up to a noble height, and lording it over the surrounding country. Every change of season, every change of weather, indeed, every hour of the day, produces some change in the magical hues and shapes of these mountains, and they are regarded by all the good wives, far and near, as perfect barometers. When the weather is fair and settled, they are clothed in blue and purple, and print their bold outlines on the clear evening sky; but sometimes, when the rest of the landscape is cloudless, they will gather a hood of gray vapors about their summits, which, in the last rays of the setting sun, will glow and light up like a crown of glory.

At the foot of these fairy mountains, the voyager may have descried the light smoke curling up from a village, whose shingle-roofs gleam among the trees, just where the blue tints of the upland melt away into the fresh green of the nearer landscape. It is a little village, of great antiquity, having been founded by some of the Dutch colonists, in the early times of the province, just about the beginning of the government of the good Peter Stuyvesant (may he rest in peace!), and there were some of the houses of the original settlers standing within a few years, built of small yellow bricks brought from Holland, having latticed windows and gable fronts, surmounted with weathercocks.

In that same village, and in one of these very houses (which, to tell the precise truth, was sadly time-worn and weather-beaten), there lived many years since, while the country was yet a province of Great Britain, a simple good-natured fellow, of the name of Rip Van Winkle. He was a descendant of the Van Winkles who figured so gallantly in the chivalrous days of Peter Stuyvesant, and accompanied him to the siege of Fort Christina. He inherited, however, but little of the martial character of his ancestors. I have observed that he was a simple good-natured man; he was, moreover, a kind neighbor, and an obedient hen-pecked husband. Indeed, to the latter circumstance might be owing that meekness of spirit which gained him such universal popularity; for those men are most apt to be obsequious and conciliating abroad, who are under the discipline of shrews at home. Their tempers, doubtless, are rendered pliant and malleable in the fiery furnace of domestic tribulation, and a curtain lecture is worth all the sermons in the world for teaching the

virtues of patience and long-suffering. A termagant wife may, therefore, in some respects, be considered a tolerable blessing; and if so, Rip Van Winkle was thrice blessed.

Certain it is that he was a great favorite among all the good wives of the village, who, as usual with the amiable sex, took his part in all family squabbles; and never failed, whenever they talked those matters over in their evening gossipings, to lay all the blame on Dame Van Winkle. The children of the village, too, would shout with joy whenever he approached. He assisted at their sports, made their playthings, taught them to fly kites and shoot marbles, and told them long stories of ghosts, witches, and Indians. Whenever he went dodging about the village, he was surrounded by a troop of them hanging on his skirts, clambering on his back, and playing a thousand tricks on him with impunity; and not a dog would bark at him throughout the neighborhood.

The great error in Rip's composition was an insuperable aversion to all kinds of profitable labor. It could not be from the want of assiduity or perseverance; for he would sit on a wet rock, with a rod as long and heavy as a Tartar's lance, and fish all day without a murmur, even though he should not be encouraged by a single nibble. He would carry a fowling-piece on his shoulder for hours together, trudging through woods and swamps, and up hill and down dale, to shoot a few squirrels or wild pigeons. He would never refuse to assist a neighbor even in the

roughest toil, and was a foremost man at all country frolics for husking Indian corn, or building stone fences; the women of the village, too, used to employ him to run their errands, and to do such little odd jobs as their less obliging husbands would not do for them. In a word, Rip was ready to attend to anybody's business but his own; but as to doing family duty, and keeping his farm in order, he found it impossible.

In fact, he declared it was of no use to work on his farm; it was the most pestilent little piece of ground in the whole country; everything about it went wrong, and would go wrong, in spite of him. His fences were continually falling to pieces; his cow would either go astray, or get among the cabbages; weeds were sure to grow quicker in his fields than anywhere else; the rain always made a point of setting in just as he had some outdoor work to do; so that though his patrimonial estate had dwindled away under his management, acre by acre, until there was little more left than a mere patch of Indian corn and potatoes, yet it was the worst conditioned farm in the neighborhood.

His children, too, were as ragged and wild as if they belonged to nobody. His son Rip, an urchin begotten in his own likeness, promised to inherit the habits, with the old clothes of his father. He was generally seen trooping like a colt at his mother's heels, equipped in a pair of his father's cast-off galligaskins, which he had much ado to hold up with one hand, as a fine lady does her train in bad weather.

Rip Van Winkle, however, was one of those happy mortals, of foolish, well-oiled dispositions, who take the world easy, eat white bread or brown, whichever can be got with least thought or trouble, and would rather starve on a penny than work for a pound. If left to himself, he would have whistled life away in perfect contentment; but his wife kept continually dinning in his ears about his idleness, his carelessness, and the ruin he was bringing on his family. Morning, noon, and night, her tongue was incessantly going, and everything he said or did was sure to produce a torrent of household eloquence. Rip had but one way of replying to all lectures of the kind, and that, by frequent use, had grown into a habit. He shrugged his shoulders, shook his head, cast up his eyes, but said nothing. This, however, always provoked a fresh volley from his wife; so that he was fain to draw off his forces, and take to the outside of the house — the only side which, in truth, belongs to a hen-pecked husband.

Rip's sole domestic adherent was his dog Wolf, who was as much hen-pecked as his master; for Dame Van Winkle regarded them as compan-ions in idleness, and even looked upon Wolf with an evil eye, as the cause of his master's going so often astray. True it is, in all points of spirit befit-ting an honorable dog, he was as courageous an animal as ever scoured the woods — but what courage can withstand the ever-during and all besetting terrors of a woman's tongue? The moment Wolf entered the house, his crest fell, his tail drooped to the ground, or curled between his legs, he sneaked about with a gallows air, casting many a sidelong glance at Dame Van Winkle, and at the least flourish of a broomstick or ladle, he would fly to the door with yelping precipitation.

Times grew worse and worse with Rip Van Winkle as years of matri-mony rolled on; a tart temper never mellows with age, and a sharp tongue is the only edged tool that grows keener with constant use. For a long while he used to console himself, when driven from home, by fre-quenting a kind of perpetual club of the sages, philosophers, and other idle personages of the village; which held its sessions on a bench before a small inn, designated by a rubicund portrait of His Majesty George the

Third. Here they used to sit in the shade through a long lazy summer's day, talking listlessly over village gossip, or telling endless sleepy stories about nothing. But it would have been worth any statesman's money to have heard the profound discussions that sometimes took place, when by chance an old newspaper fell into their hands from some passing traveler. How solemnly they would listen to the contents, as drawled out by Derrick Van Bummel, the schoolmaster, a dapper learned little man, who was not to be daunted by the most gigantic word in the dictionary; and how sagely they would deliberate upon public events some months after they had taken place.

The opinions of this junto were completely controlled by Nicholas Vedder, a patriarch of the village, and landlord of the inn, at the door of which he took his seat from morning till night, just moving sufficiently to avoid the sun and keep in the shade of a large tree; so that the neighbors could tell the hour by his movements as accurately as by a sundial. It is true he was rarely heard to speak, but smoked his pipe incessantly. His adherents, however (for every great man has his adherents), perfectly understood him, and knew how to gather his opinions. When anything that was read or related displeased him, he was observed to smoke his pipe vehemently, and to send forth short, frequent, and angry puffs; but when pleased, he would inhale the smoke slowly and tranquilly, and emit it in light and placid clouds; and sometimes, taking the pipe from his mouth, and letting the fragrant vapor curl about his nose, would gravely nod his head in token of perfect approbation.

From even this stronghold the unlucky Rip was at length routed by his termagant wife, who would suddenly break in upon the tranquillity of the assemblage and call the members all to naught; nor was that august personage, Nicholas Vedder himself, sacred from the daring tongue of this terrible virago, who charged him outright with encouraging her husband in habits of idleness.

Poor Rip was at last reduced almost to despair; and his only alternative, to escape from the labor of the farm and clamor of his wife, was to take gun in hand and stroll away into the woods. Here he would sometimes seat himself at the foot of a tree, and share the contents of his wallet with Wolf, with whom he sympathized as a fellow-sufferer in persecution. "Poor Wolf," he would say, "thy mistress leads thee a dog's life of it; but never mind, my lad, whilst I live thou shalt never want a friend to stand by thee!" Wolf would wag his tail, look wistfully in his master's face, and if dogs can feel pity, I verily believe he reciprocated the sentiment with all his heart.

In a long ramble of the kind on a fine autumnal day, Rip had unconsciously scrambled to one of the highest parts of the Kaatskill mountains. He was after his favorite sport of squirrel-shooting, and the still solitudes had echoed and re-echoed with the reports of his gun. Panting and fatigued, he threw himself, late in the afternoon, on a green knoll, covered with mountain herbage, that crowned the brow of a precipice. From an opening between the trees he could overlook all the lower country for many a mile of rich woodland. He saw at a distance the lordly Hudson, far, far below him, moving on its silent but majestic course, with the reflection of a purple cloud, or the sail of a lagging bark, here and there sleeping on its glassy bosom, and at last losing itself in the blue highlands.

On the other side he looked down into a deep mountain glen, wild, lonely, and shagged, the bottom filled with fragments from the impending cliffs, and scarcely lighted by the reflecting rays of the setting sun. For some time Rip lay musing on this scene; evening was gradually advancing; the mountains began to throw their long blue shadows over the valleys; he saw that it would be dark long before he could reach the village, and he heaved a heavy sigh when he thought of encountering the terrors of Dame Van Winkle.

As he was about to descend, he heard a voice from a distance, halloing, "Rip Van Winkle! Rip Van Winkle!" He looked round but could see nothing but a crow winging its solitary flight across the mountain. He thought his fancy must have deceived him, and turned again to descend, when he heard the same cry ring through the still evening air; "Rip Van Winkle! Rip Van Winkle!" — at the same time Wolf bristled up his back, and, giving a low growl, skulked to his master's side, looking fearfully down into the glen. Rip now felt a vague apprehension stealing over him; he looked anxiously in the same direction, and perceived a strange figure slowly toiling up the rocks, and bending under the weight of something he carried on his back. He was surprised to see any human being in this lonely and unfrequented place; but supposing it to be someone of the neighborhood in need of his assistance, he hastened down to yield it.

On nearer approach, he was still more surprised at the singularity of the stranger's appearance. He was a short, square-built old fellow, with thick bushy hair, and a grizzled beard. His dress was of the antique Dutch fashion — a cloth jerkin, strapped round the waist — several pairs of breeches, the outer one of ample volume, decorated with rows of buttons down the sides, and bunches at the knees. He bore on his shoulder a stout keg, that seemed full of liquor, and made signs for Rip to approach and assist him with the load. Though rather shy and distrustful of this new acquaintance, Rip complied with his usual alacrity; and mutually relieving each other, they clambered up a narrow gully, apparently the dry bed of a mountain torrent. As they ascended, Rip

every now and then heard long rolling peals, like distant thunder, that seemed to issue out of a deep ravine, or rather cleft, between lofty rocks, toward which their rugged path conducted. He paused for an instant, but supposing it to be the muttering of one of those transient thunder-showers which often take place in mountain heights, he proceeded. Passing through the ravine, they came to a hollow, like a small amphitheater, surrounded by perpendicular precipices, over the brinks of which impending trees shot their branches, so that you only caught glimpses of the azure sky and the bright evening cloud. During the whole time Rip and his companion had labored on in silence, for though the former marveled greatly what could be the object of carrying a keg of liquor up this wild mountain, yet there was something strange and incomprehensible about the unknown, that inspired awe and checked familiarity.

On entering the amphitheater, new objects of wonder presented themselves. On a level spot in the center was a company of odd-looking personages playing at ninepins. They were dressed in a quaint outlandish fashion; some wore short doublets, others jerkins, with long knives in their belts, and most of them had enormous breeches, of similar style with that of the guide's. Their visages, too, were peculiar; one had a large head, broad face, and small piggish eyes; the face of another seemed to consist entirely of nose, and was surmounted by a white sugar-loaf hat, set off with a little red cock's tail. They all had beards, of various shapes and colors. There was one who seemed to be the commander. He was a stout old gentleman, with a weather-beaten countenance; he wore a laced doublet, broad belt and hanger, high-crowned hat and feather, red stockings, and high-heeled shoes, with roses in them. The whole group reminded Rip of the figures in an old Flemish painting, in the parlor of Dominie Van Shaick, the village parson, and which had been brought over from Holland at the time of the settlement.

What seemed particularly odd to Rip was, that though these folks were evidently amusing themselves, yet they maintained the gravest faces, the most mysterious silence, and were, withal, the most melancholy

party of pleasure he had ever witnessed. Nothing interrupted the stillness of the scene but the noise of the balls, which, whenever they were rolled, echoed along the mountains like rumbling peals of thunder.

As Rip and his companion approached them, they suddenly desisted from their play, and stared at him with such fixed, statue-like gazes, and such strange, uncouth, lackluster countenances, that his heart turned within him, and his knees smote together. His companion now emptied the contents of the keg into large flagons, and made signs to him to wait upon the company. He obeyed with fear and trembling; they quaffed the liquor in profound silence, and then returned to their game.

By degrees Rip's awe and apprehension subsided. He even ventured, when no eye was fixed upon him, to taste the beverage, which he found had much of the flavor of excellent Hollands. He was naturally a thirsty soul, and was soon tempted to repeat the draught. One taste provoked another; and he reiterated his visits to the flagon so often, that at length his senses were overpowered, his eyes swam in his head, his head gradually declined, and he fell into a deep sleep.

On waking, he found himself on the green knoll whence he had first seen the old man of the glen. He rubbed his eyes — it was a bright sunny morning. The birds were hopping and twittering among the bushes, and the eagle was wheeling aloft, and breasting the pure mountain breeze. "Surely," thought Rip, "I have not slept here all night." He recalled the occurrences before he fell asleep. The strange man with a keg of liquor — the mountain ravine — the wild retreat among the rocks — the woebegone party at ninepins — the flagon — "Oh! That flagon! that wicked flagon!" thought Rip; "What excuse shall I make to Dame Van Winkle?"

He looked round for his gun, but in place of the clean well-oiled fowling-piece, he found an old firelock lying by him, the barrel incrusted with rust, the lock falling off, and the stock worm-eaten. He now suspected that the grave roysters of the mountain had put a trick upon him, and, having dosed him with liquor, had robbed him of his gun. Wolf, too, had disappeared, but he might have strayed away after a squirrel or partridge. He whistled after him, and shouted his name, but all in vain; the echoes repeated his whistle and shout, but no dog was to be seen.

He determined to revisit the scene of the last evening's gambol, and, if he met with any of the party, to demand his dog and gun. As he rose to walk, he found himself stiff in the joints, and wanting in his usual activity. "These mountain beds do not agree with me," thought Rip, "and if this frolic should lay me up with a fit of the rheumatism, I shall have a blessed time with Dame Van Winkle." With some difficulty he got down into the glen: he found the gully up which he and his companion had ascended the preceding evening; but, to his astonishment, a mountain stream was now foaming down it — leaping from rock to rock, and filling the glen with babbling murmurs. He, however, made shift to scramble up its sides, working his toilsome way through thickets of birch, sassafras, and witch-hazel, and sometimes tripped up or entangled by the wild grapevines that twisted their coils or tendrils from tree to tree, and spread a kind of network in his path.

At length he reached to where the ravine had opened through the cliffs to the amphitheater; but no traces of such opening remained. The rocks presented a high impenetrable wall, over which the torrent came tumbling in a sheet of feathery foam, and fell into a broad, deep basin, black from the shadows of the surrounding forest. Here, then, poor Rip was brought to a stand. He again called and whistled after his dog; he was only answered by the cawing of a flock of idle crows, sporting high in air about a dry tree that overhung a sunny precipice; and who, secure in their elevation, seemed to look down and scoff at the poor man's perplexities. What was to be done? The morning was passing away, and Rip felt famished for want of his breakfast. He grieved to give up his dog and his gun; he dreaded to meet his wife; but it would not do to starve among the mountains. He shook his head, shouldered the rusty firelock, and, with a heart full of trouble and anxiety, turned his steps homeward.

As he approached the village he met a number of people, but none whom he knew, which somewhat surprised him, for he had thought himself acquainted with everyone in the country round. Their dress, too, was of a different fashion from that to which he was accustomed. They all stared at him with equal marks of surprise, and, whenever they cast their eyes upon him, invariably stroked their chins. The constant recurrence of this gesture induced Rip, involuntarily, to do the same — when, to his astonishment, he found his beard had grown a foot long!

He had now entered the skirts of the village. A troop of strange children ran at his heels, hooting after him, and pointing at his gray beard. The dogs, too, not one of which he recognized for an old acquaintance, barked at him as he passed. The very village was altered; it was larger and more populous. There were rows of houses which he had never seen before, and those which had been his familiar haunts had disappeared. Strange names were over the doors — strange faces at the windows — everything was strange. His mind now misgave him; he began to doubt whether both he and the world around him were not bewitched. Surely this was his native village, which he had left but the day before. There stood the Kaatskill mountains — there ran the silver Hudson at a distance — there was every hill and dale precisely as it had always been. Rip was sorely perplexed. "That flagon last night," thought he, "has addled my poor head sadly!"

It was with some difficulty that he found the way to his own house, which he approached with silent awe, expecting every moment to hear the shrill voice of Dame Van Winkle. He found the house gone to decay — the roof fallen in, the windows shattered, and the doors off the hinges. A half-starved dog that looked like Wolf was skulking about it. Rip called him by name, but the cur snarled, showed his teeth, and passed on. This was an unkind cut indeed — "My very dog," sighed poor Rip, "has forgotten me!"

He entered the house, which, to tell the truth, Dame Van Winkle had always kept in neat order. It was empty, forlorn, and apparently abandoned. The desolateness overcame all his connubial fears — he called loudly for his wife and children — the lonely chambers rang for a moment with his voice, and then all again was silence.

He now hurried forth, and hastened to his old resort, the village inn — but it too was gone. A large, rickety, wooden building stood in its place, with great gaping windows, some of them broken and mended with old hats and petticoats, and over the door was painted, "The Union Hotel, by Jonathan Doolittle." Instead of the great tree that used to shelter the quiet little Dutch inn of yore, there was now reared a tall naked pole, with something on the top that looked like a red nightcap, and from it was fluttering a flag, on which was a singular assemblage of stars and stripes — all this was strange and incomprehensible. He recognized on the sign, however, the ruby face of King George, under which he had smoked so many a peaceful pipe; but even this was singularly metamorphosed. The red coat was changed for one of blue and buff, a sword was held in the hand instead of a scepter, the head was decorated with a cocked hat, and underneath was painted in large characters, GENERAL WASHINGTON.

There was, as usual, a crowd of folk about the door, but none that Rip recollected. The very character of the people seemed changed. There was a busy, bustling, disputatious tone about it, instead of the accustomed phlegm and drowsy tranquillity. He looked in vain for the sage Nicholas Vedder, with his broad face, double chin, and fair long pipe, uttering clouds of tobacco-smoke instead of idle speeches; or Van Bummel, the schoolmaster, doling forth the contents of an ancient newspaper. In place of these, a lean, bilious-looking fellow, with his pockets full of hand-bills, was haranguing vehemently about rights of citizens — elections — members of Congress — liberty — Bunker's Hill — heroes of seventy-six — and other words, which were a perfect Babylonish jargon to the bewildered Van Winkle.

The appearance of Rip, with his long grizzled beard, his rusty fowling-piece, his uncouth dress, and an army of women and children at his heels, soon attracted the attention of the tavern politicians. They crowded round him, eyeing him from head to foot with great curiosity. The orator bustled up to him, and, drawing him partly aside, inquired "on which side he voted?" Rip stared in vacant stupidity. Another short but busy

little fellow pulled him by the arm, and, rising on tiptoe, inquired in his ear, "Whether he was Federal or Democrat?" Rip was equally at a loss to comprehend the question; when a knowing, self-important old gentleman, in a sharp cocked hat, made his way through the crowd, putting them to the right and left with his elbows as he passed, and planting himself before Van Winkle, with one arm akimbo, the other resting on his cane, his keen eyes and sharp hat penetrating, as it were, into his very soul, demanded in an austere tone, "what brought him to the election with a gun on his shoulder, and a mob at his heels, and whether he meant to breed a riot in the village?" — "Alas! Gentlemen," cried Rip, somewhat dismayed, "I am a poor quiet man, a native of this place, and a loyal subject of the king, God bless him!"

Here a general shout burst from the bystanders — "A tory! A tory! A spy! A refugee! Hustle him! Away with him!" It was with great difficulty that the self-important man in the cocked hat restored order; and, having assumed a tenfold austerity of brow, demanded again of the unknown culprit, what he came there for, and whom he was seeking? The poor man humbly assured him that he meant no harm, but merely came there in search of some of his neighbors, who used to keep about the tavern.

"Well — who are they? — name them."

Rip bethought himself a moment, and inquired, "Where's Nicholas Vedder?"

There was a silence for a little while, when an old man replied in a thin piping voice, "Nicholas Vedder! Why, he is dead and gone these eighteen years! There was a wooden tombstone in the churchyard that used to tell about him, but that's rotten and gone too."

"Where's Brom Dutcher?"

"Oh, he went off to the army in the beginning of the war; some say he was killed at the storming of Stony Point — others say he was drowned in a squall at the foot of Antony's Nose. I don't know — he never came back again."

"Where's Van Bummel, the schoolmaster?"

"He went off to the wars too, was a great militia general, and is now in Congress."

Rip's heart died away at hearing of these sad changes in his home and friends, and finding himself thus alone in the world. Every answer puzzled him too, by treating of such enormous lapses of time, and of matters which he could not understand: war — Congress — Stony Point; — he had no courage to ask after any more friends, but cried out in despair, "Does nobody here know Rip Van Winkle?"

"Oh, Rip Van Winkle!" exclaimed two or three. "Oh, to be sure! that's Rip Van Winkle yonder, leaning against the tree."

Rip looked, and beheld a precise counterpart of himself, as he went up the mountain: apparently as lazy, and certainly as ragged. The poor fellow was now completely confounded. He doubted his own identity, and whether he was himself or another man. In the midst of his bewilderment, the man in the cocked hat demanded who he was, and what was his name?

"God knows," exclaimed he, at his wits' end; "I'm not myself — I'm somebody else — that's me yonder — no — that's somebody else got into my shoes — I was myself last night, but I fell asleep on the mountain, and they've changed my gun, and everything's changed, and I'm changed, and I can't tell what's my name, or who I am!"

The bystanders began now to look at each other, nod, wink significantly, and tap their fingers against their foreheads. There was a whisper, also, about securing the gun, and keeping the old fellow from doing mischief, at the very suggestion of which the self-important man in the cocked hat retired with some precipitation. At this critical moment a fresh, comely woman pressed through the throng to get a peep at the gray-bearded man. She had a chubby child in her arms, which, frightened at his looks, began to cry. "Hush, Rip," cried she, "hush, you little fool; the old man won't hurt you." The name of the child, the air of the mother, the tone of her voice, all awakened a train of recollections in his mind.

"What is your name, my good woman?" asked he.

"Judith Gardenier."

"And your father's name?"

"Ah, poor man, Rip Van Winkle was his name, but it's twenty years since he went away from home with his gun, and never has been heard of since — his dog came home without him; but whether he shot himself, or was carried away by the Indians, nobody can tell. I was then but a little girl."

Rip had but one question more to ask; but he put it with a faltering voice: "Where's your mother?"

"Oh, she too had died but a short time since; she broke a blood-vessel in a fit of passion at a New-England peddler."

There was a drop of comfort, at least, in this intelligence. The honest man could contain himself no longer. He caught his daughter and her child in his arms. "I am your father!" cried he — "Young Rip Van Winkle once — old Rip Van Winkle now! — Does nobody know poor Rip Van Winkle?"

All stood amazed, until an old woman, tottering out from among the crowd, put her hand to her brow, and peering under it in his face for a moment, exclaimed, "Sure enough! It is Rip Van Winkle — It is himself! Welcome home again, old neighbor — Why, where have you been these twenty long years?"

Rip's story was soon told, for the whole twenty years had been to him but as one night. The neighbors stared when they heard it; some were seen to wink at each other, and put their tongues in their cheeks: and the self-important man in the cocked hat, who, when the alarm was over, had returned to the field, screwed down the corners of his mouth, and shook his head — upon which there was a general shaking of the head throughout the assemblage.

It was determined, however, to take the opinion of old Peter Vanderdonk, who was seen slowly advancing up the road. He was a descendant of the historian of that name, who wrote one of the earliest accounts of the province. Peter was the most ancient inhabitant of the village, and well versed in all the wonderful events and traditions of the neighborhood. He recollected Rip at once, and corroborated his story in the most satisfactory manner. He assured the company that it was a fact, handed down from his ancestor the historian, that the Kaatskill mountains had always been haunted by strange beings. That it was affirmed that the great Hendrick Hudson, the first discoverer of the river and country, kept a kind of vigil there every twenty years, with his crew of the *Half-moon*; being permitted in this way to revisit the scenes of his enterprise, and keep a guardian eye upon the river, and the great city called by his name. That his father had once seen them in their old Dutch dresses playing at ninepins in a hollow of the mountain; and that he himself had heard, one summer afternoon, the sound of their balls, like distant peals of thunder.

To make a long story short, the company broke up, and returned to the more important concerns of the election. Rip's daughter took him home to live with her; she had a snug, well-furnished house, and a stout cheery farmer for a husband, whom Rip recollected for one of the urchins that used to climb upon his back. As to Rip's son and heir, who was the ditto of himself, seen leaning against the tree, he was employed to work on the farm; but evinced an hereditary disposition to attend to anything else but his business.

Rip now resumed his old walks and habits; he soon found many of his former cronies, though all rather the worse for the wear and tear of time; and preferred making friends among the rising generation, with whom he soon grew into great favor.

Having nothing to do at home, and being arrived at that happy age when a man can be idle with impunity, he took his place once more on the bench at the inn door, and was reverenced as one of the patriarchs of the village, and a chronicle of the old times "before the war." It was some time before he could get into the regular track of gossip, or could be made to comprehend the strange events that had taken place during his torpor. How that there had been a revolutionary war — that the country had thrown off the yoke of old England — and that, instead of being a subject of His Majesty George the Third, he was now a free citizen of the United States. Rip, in fact, was no politician; the changes of states and empires made but little impression on him; but there was one species of despotism under which he had long groaned, and that was — petticoat government. Happily that was at an end; he had got his neck out of the yoke of matrimony, and could go in and out whenever he pleased without dreading the tyranny of Dame Van Winkle. Whenever her name was mentioned, however, he shook his head, shrugged his shoulders, and cast up his eyes; which might pass either for an expression of resignation to his fate, or joy at his deliverance.

He used to tell his story to every stranger that arrived at Mr. Doolittle's hotel. He was observed, at first, to vary on some points every time he told it, which was, doubtless, owing to his having so recently awaked. It at last settled down precisely to the tale I have related, and not a man, woman, or child in the neighborhood but knew it by heart. Some always pretended to doubt the reality of it, and insisted that Rip had been out of his head, and that this was one point on which he always remained flighty. The old Dutch inhabitants, however, almost universally gave it full credit. Even to this day they never hear a thunderstorm of a summer afternoon about the Kaatskill, but they say Hendrick Hudson and his crew are at their game of ninepins; and it is a common wish of all henpecked husbands in the neighborhood, when life hangs heavy on their hands, that they might have a quieting draught out of Rip Van Winkle's flagon.

FEATHERTOP

NATHANIEL HAWTHORNE

❧ Nathaniel Hawthorne (1804–64) was born in Salem, Massachusetts. One of his ancestors was a judge at the infamous Salem witchcraft trials, who would have quickly recognized Mother Rigby, and made a shrewd guess as to what fire was the source of the coals with which she lit her pipe. "Feathertop" is therefore rooted firmly in the folklore and superstitions of New England. However, despite Hawthorne's claim that the tale is "one which I heard on my grandmother's knee," it is probably not founded on a genuine legend. In its mixture of pathos and humor, this story, first published in the **International Monthly Magazine** *(1852), shows Hawthorne's genius at its best; it may be compared in some respects both with Mary Shelley's* **Frankenstein** *(1818), and Hans Christian Andersen's "The Shadow" (1847). Feathertop himself, as the critic Brian Attebery has pointed out, came back to life as "Jack Pumpkinhead" in L. Frank Baum's Oz books. Hawthorne's major works include the novels* **The Scarlet Letter** *(1850) and* **The House of the Seven Gables** *(1851), and, for children,* **A Wonder Book** *(1852) and* **Tanglewood Tales** *(1853). His son Julian Hawthorne (1846–1934) also wrote fairy tales for children, most successfully in the volume* **Yellow-Cap and Other Fairy-Stories for Children** *(1880). ❦*

"DICKON," CRIED Mother Rigby, "a coal for my pipe!"

The pipe was in the old dame's mouth when she said these words. She had thrust it there after filling it with tobacco, but without stooping to light it at the hearth, where indeed there was no appearance of a

fire having been kindled that morning. Forthwith, however, as soon as the order was given, there was an intense red glow out of the bowl of the pipe, and a whiff of smoke from Mother Rigby's lips. Whence the coal came, and how brought thither by an invisible hand, I have never been able to discover.

"Good!" quoth Mother Rigby, with a nod of her head. "Thank ye, Dickon! And now for making this scarecrow. Be within call, Dickon, in case I need you again."

The good woman had risen thus early (for as yet it was scarcely sunrise) in order to set about making a scarecrow, which she intended to put in the middle of her corn-patch. It was now the latter week of May, and the crows and blackbirds had already discovered the little, green, rolled-up leaf of the Indian corn just peeping out of the soil. She was determined, therefore, to contrive as lifelike a scarecrow as ever was seen, and to finish it immediately, from top to toe, so that it should begin its sentinel's duty that very morning. Now, Mother Rigby (as everybody must have heard) was one of the most cunning and potent witches in New England, and might, with very little trouble, have made a scarecrow ugly enough to frighten the minister himself. But on this occasion, as she had awakened in an uncommonly pleasant humor, and was further dulcified by her pipe of tobacco, she resolved to produce something fine, beautiful, and splendid, rather than hideous and horrible.

"I don't want to set up a hobgoblin in my own corn-patch, and almost at my own doorstep," said Mother Rigby to herself, puffing out a whiff of smoke. "I could do it if I pleased, but I'm tired of doing marvelous things, and so I'll keep within the bounds of everyday business, just for variety's sake. Besides, there's no use in scaring the little children for a mile roundabout, though 'tis true I'm a witch."

It was settled, therefore, in her own mind, that the scarecrow should represent a fine gentleman of the period, so far as the materials at hand would allow. Perhaps it may be as well to enumerate the chief of the articles that went to the composition of this figure.

The most important item of all, probably, although it made so little show, was a certain broomstick, on which Mother Rigby had taken many an airy gallop at midnight, and which now served the scarecrow by way of a spinal column, or, as the unlearned phrase it, a backbone. One of its arms was a disabled flail which used to be wielded by Goodman Rigby, before his spouse worried him out of this troublesome world; the other, if I mistake not, was composed of the pudding stick and a broken rung of a chair, tied loosely together at the elbow. As for its legs, the right was a hoe handle, and the left an undistinguished and miscellaneous stick from the woodpile. Its lungs, stomach, and other affairs of that kind were nothing better than a meal bag stuffed with straw. Thus we have made out the skeleton and entire corporosity of the scarecrow, with the exception of its head; and this was admirably supplied by a somewhat withered and shriveled pumpkin, in which Mother Rigby cut two holes for the eyes, and a slit for the mouth, leaving a bluish-colored knob in the middle to pass for a nose. It was really quite a respectable face.

"I've seen worse ones on human shoulders, at any rate," said Mother Rigby. "And many a fine gentleman has a pumpkin head, as well as my scarecrow."

But the clothes, in this case, were to be the making of the man. So the good old woman took down from a peg an ancient plum-colored coat of

London make, and with relics of embroidery on its seams, cuffs, pocket-flaps, and button-holes, but lamentably worn and faded, patched at the elbows, tattered at the skirts, and threadbare all over. On the left breast was a round hole, whence either a star of nobility had been rent away, or else the hot heart of some former wearer had scorched it through and through. The neighbors said that this rich garment belonged to the Black Man's* wardrobe, and that he kept it at Mother Rigby's cottage for the convenience of slipping it on whenever he wished to make a grand appearance at the governor's table. To match the coat there was a velvet waistcoat of very ample size, and formerly embroidered with foliage that had been as brightly golden as the maple leaves in October, but which had now quite vanished out of the substance of the velvet. Next came a pair of scarlet breeches, once worn by the French governor of Louisbourg, and the knees of which had touched the lower step of the throne of Louis le Grand. The Frenchman had given these small-clothes to an Indian powwow, who parted with them to the old witch for a gill of strong waters, at one of their dances in the forest. Furthermore, Mother Rigby produced a pair of silk stockings and put them on the figure's legs, where they showed as unsubstantial as a dream, with the wooden reality of the two sticks making itself miserably apparent through the holes. Lastly, she put her dead husband's wig on the bare scalp of the pumpkin, and surmounted the whole with a dusty three-cornered hat, in which was stuck the longest tail feather of a rooster.

Then the old dame stood the figure up in a corner of her cottage and chuckled to behold its yellow semblance of a visage, with its knobby little nose thrust into the air. It had a strangely self-satisfied aspect, and seemed to say, "Come look at me!"

"And you are well worth looking at, that's a fact!" quoth Mother Rigby, in admiration at her own handiwork. "I've made many a puppet since I've been a witch, but methinks this is the finest of them all. 'Tis almost too good for a scarecrow. And, by the by, I'll just fill a fresh pipe of tobacco and then take him out to the corn-patch."

* the devil

While filling her pipe the old woman continued to gaze with almost motherly affection at the figure in the corner. To say the truth, whether it were chance, or skill, or downright witchcraft, there was something wonderfully human in this ridiculous shape, bedizened with its tattered finery; and as for the countenance, it appeared to shrivel its yellow surface into a grin — a funny kind of expression betwixt scorn and merriment, as if it understood itself to be a jest at mankind. The more Mother Rigby looked, the better she was pleased.

"Dickon," cried she sharply, "another coal for my pipe!"

Hardly had she spoken, than, just as before, there was a red-glowing coal on the top of the tobacco. She drew in a long whiff and puffed it forth again into the bar of morning sunshine which struggled through the one dusty pane of her cottage window. Mother Rigby always liked to flavor her pipe with a coal of fire from the particular chimney corner whence this had been brought. But where that chimney corner might be, or who brought the coal from it — further than that the invisible messenger seemed to respond to the name of Dickon — I cannot tell.

"That puppet yonder," thought Mother Rigby, still with her eyes fixed on the scarecrow, "is too good a piece of work to stand all summer in a corn-patch, frightening away the crows and blackbirds. He's capable of better things. Why, I've danced with a worse one, when partners happened to be scarce, at our witch meetings in the forest! What if I should let him take his chance among the other men of straw and empty fellows who go bustling about the world?"

The old witch took three or four more whiffs of her pipe and smiled.

"He'll meet plenty of his brethren at every street corner!" continued she. "Well; I didn't mean to dabble in witchcraft today, further than the lighting of my pipe, but a witch I am, and a witch I'm likely to be, and there's no use trying to shirk it. I'll make a man of my scarecrow, were it only for the joke's sake!"

While muttering these words, Mother Rigby took the pipe from her own mouth and thrust it into the crevice which represented the same feature in the pumpkin visage of the scarecrow.

"Puff, darling, puff!" said she. "Puff away, my fine fellow! Your life depends on it!"

This was a strange exhortation, undoubtedly, to be addressed to a mere thing of sticks, straw, and old clothes, with nothing better than a shriveled pumpkin for a head — as we know to have been the scarecrow's case. Nevertheless, as we must carefully hold in remembrance, Mother Rigby was a witch of singular power and dexterity; and, keeping this fact duly before our minds, we shall see nothing beyond credibility in the remarkable incidents of our story. Indeed, the great difficulty will be at once got over, if we can only bring ourselves to believe that, as soon as the old dame bade him puff, there came a whiff of smoke from the scarecrow's mouth. It was the very feeblest of whiffs, to be sure; but it was followed by another and another, each more decided than the preceding one.

"Puff away, my pet! Puff away, my pretty one!" Mother Rigby kept repeating, with her pleasantest smile. "It is the breath of life to ye; and that you may take my word for."

Beyond all question the pipe was bewitched. There must have been a spell either in the tobacco or in the fiercely glowing coal that so mysteriously burned on top of it, or in the pungently aromatic smoke which exhaled from the kindled weed. The figure, after a few doubtful attempts, at length blew forth a volley of smoke extending all the way from the obscure corner into the bar of sunshine. There it eddied and melted away among the motes of dust. It seemed a convulsive effort; for the two or three next whiffs were fainter, although the coal still glowed and threw a gleam over the scarecrow's visage. The old witch clapped her skinny palms together, and smiled encouragingly upon her handiwork. She saw that the charm worked well. The shriveled, yellow face, which heretofore had been no face at all, had already a thin, fantastic haze, as it were of human likeness, shifting to and fro across it; sometimes vanishing entirely, but growing more perceptible than ever with the next whiff from the pipe. The whole figure, in like manner, assumed a show of life, such as we impart to ill-defined shapes among the clouds, and half deceive ourselves with the pastime of our own fancy.

If we must needs pry closely into the matter, it may be doubted whether there was any real change, after all, in the sordid, worn-out, worthless, and ill-joined substance of the scarecrow; but merely a spectral illusion, and a cunning effect of light and shade so colored and contrived as to delude the eyes of most men. The miracles of witchcraft seem always to have had a very shallow subtlety; and, at least, if the above explanation does not hit the truth of the process, I can suggest no better.

"Well puffed, my pretty lad!" still cried old Mother Rigby. "Come, another good stout whiff, and let it be with might and main. Puff for thy life, I tell thee! Puff out of the very bottom of thy heart, if any heart thou hast, or any bottom to it! Well done, again! Thou didst suck in that mouthful as if for the pure love of it."

And then the witch beckoned to the scarecrow, throwing so much magnetic potency into her gesture that it seemed as if it must inevitably be obeyed, like the mystic call of the loadstone when it summons the iron.

"Why lurkest thou in the corner, lazy one?" said she. "Step forth! Thou hast the world before thee!"

Upon my word, if the legend were not one which I heard on my grandmother's knee, and which had established its place among things credible before my childish judgment could analyze its probability, I question whether I should have the face to tell it now.

In obedience to Mother Rigby's word, and extending its arm as if to reach her outstretched hand, the figure made a step forward — a kind of hitch and jerk, however, rather than a step — then tottered and almost lost its balance. What could the witch expect? It was nothing, after all, but a scarecrow stuck upon two sticks. But the strong-willed old beldam scowled, and beckoned, and flung the energy of her purpose so forcibly at this poor combination of rotten wood, and musty straw, and ragged garments, that it was compelled to show itself a man, in spite of the reality of things. So it stepped into the bar of sunshine. There it stood — poor devil of a contrivance that it was! — with only the thinnest vesture of human similitude about it, through which was evident the stiff, rickety, incongruous, faded, tattered, good-for-nothing patchwork of its substance, ready to sink in a heap upon the floor, as if conscious of its own unworthiness to be erect. Shall I confess the truth? At its present point of vivification, the scarecrow reminds me of some of the lukewarm and abortive characters, composed of heterogeneous materials, used for the thousandth time, and never worth using, with which romance writers (and myself, no doubt, among the rest) have so overpeopled the world of fiction.

But the fierce old hag began to get angry and show a glimpse of her diabolic nature (like a snake's head, peeping with a hiss out of her bosom), at this pusillanimous behavior of the thing which she had taken the trouble to put together.

"Puff away, wretch!" cried she, wrathfully. "Puff, puff, puff, thou thing of straw and emptiness! Thou rag or two! Thou meal bag! Thou pumpkin head! Thou nothing! Where shall I find a name vile enough to call thee by? Puff, I say, and suck in thy fantastic life with the smoke! Else I snatch the pipe from thy mouth and hurl thee where that red coal came from."

Thus threatened, the unhappy scarecrow had nothing for it but to puff away for dear life. As need was, therefore, it applied itself lustily to the pipe and sent forth such abundant volleys of tobacco smoke that the small cottage kitchen became all vaporous. The one sunbeam struggled mistily through, and could but imperfectly define the image of the cracked and dusty window pane on the opposite wall. Mother Rigby, meanwhile, with one brown arm akimbo and the other stretched toward the figure, loomed grimly amid the obscurity with such port and expression as when she was wont to heave a ponderous nightmare on her victims and stand at the bedside to enjoy their agony. In fear and trembling did this poor scarecrow puff. But its efforts, it must be acknowledged, served an excellent purpose; for, with each successive whiff, the figure lost more and more of its dizzy and perplexing tenuity and seemed to take denser substance. Its very garments, moreover, partook of the magical change, and shone with the gloss of novelty, and glistened with the skillfully embroidered gold that had long ago been rent away. And, half revealed among the smoke, a yellow visage bent its lusterless eyes on Mother Rigby.

At last the old witch clinched her fist and shook it at the figure. Not that she was positively angry, but merely acting on the principle — perhaps untrue, or not the only truth, though as high a one as Mother Rigby could be expected to attain — that feeble and torpid natures, being incapable of better inspiration, must be stirred up by fear. But here was the crisis. Should she fail in what she now sought to effect, it was her ruthless purpose to scatter the miserable simulacre into its original elements.

"Thou hast a man's aspect," said she, sternly. "Have also the echo and mockery of a voice! I bid thee speak!"

The scarecrow gasped, struggled, and at length emitted a murmur, which was so incorporated with its smoky breath that you could scarcely tell whether it were indeed a voice or only a whiff of tobacco. Some narrators of this legend hold the opinion that Mother Rigby's conjurations and the fierceness of her will had compelled a familiar spirit into the figure, and that the voice was his.

"Mother," mumbled the poor stifled voice, "be not so awful with me! I would fain speak; but being without wits, what can I say?"

"Thou canst speak, darling, canst thou?" cried Mother Rigby, relaxing her grim countenance into a smile. "And what shalt thou say, quotha! Say, indeed! Art thou of the brotherhood of the empty skull, and demandest of me what thou shalt say? Thou shalt say a thousand things, and saying them a thousand times over, thou shalt still have said nothing! Be not afraid, I tell thee! When thou comest into the world (whither I purpose sending thee forthwith) thou shalt not lack the wherewithal to talk. Talk! Why, thou shalt babble like a mill-stream, if thou wilt. Thou hast brains enough for that, I trow!"

"At your service, mother," responded the figure.

"And that was well said, my pretty one," answered Mother Rigby. "Then thou spakest like thyself, and meant nothing. Thou shalt have a hundred such set phrases, and five hundred to the boot of them. And now, darling, I have taken so much pains with thee and thou art so beautiful, that, by my troth, I love thee better than any witch's puppet in the world; and I've made them of all sorts — clay, wax, straw, sticks, night fog, morning mist, sea foam, and chimney smoke. But thou art the very best. So give heed to what I say."

"Yes, kind mother," said the figure, "with all my heart!"

"With all thy heart!" cried the old witch, setting her hands to her sides and laughing loudly. "Thou hast such a pretty way of speaking. With all thy heart! And thou didst put thy hand to the left side of thy waistcoat as if thou really hadst one!"

So now, in high good humor with this fantastic contrivance of hers, Mother Rigby told the scarecrow that it must go and play its part in the great world, where not one man in a hundred, she affirmed, was gifted with more real substance than itself. And, that he might hold up his head with the best of them, she endowed him, on the spot, with an unreckonable amount of wealth. It consisted partly of a gold mine in Eldorado, and of ten thousand shares in a broken bubble, and of half a million acres of vineyard at the North Pole, and of a castle in the air, and a château in Spain, together with all the rents and income therefrom accruing. She further made over to him the cargo of a certain ship, laden with salt of

Cadiz, which she herself, by her necromantic arts, had caused to founder, ten years before, in the deepest part of mid-ocean. If the salt were not dissolved, and could be brought to market, it would fetch a pretty penny among the fishermen. That he might not lack ready money, she gave him a copper farthing of Birmingham manufacture, being all the coin she had about her, and likewise a great deal of brass, which she applied to his forehead, thus making it yellower than ever.

"With that brass alone," quoth Mother Rigby, "thou canst pay thy way all over the earth. Kiss me, pretty darling! I have done my best for thee."

Furthermore, that the adventurer might lack no possible advantage toward a fair start in life, this excellent old dame gave him a token by which he was to introduce himself to a certain magistrate, member of the council, merchant, and elder of the church (the four capacities constituting but one man), who stood at the head of society in the neighboring metropolis. The token was neither more nor less than a single word, which Mother Rigby whispered to the scarecrow, and which the scarecrow was to whisper to the merchant.

"Gouty as the old fellow is, he'll run thy errands for thee, when once thou hast given him that word in his ear," said the old witch. "Mother Rigby knows the worshipful Justice Gookin, and the worshipful Justice knows Mother Rigby!"

Here the witch thrust her wrinkled face close to the puppet's, chuckling irrepressibly, and fidgeting all through her system, with delight at the idea which she meant to communicate.

"The worshipful Master Gookin," whispered she, "hath a comely maiden to his daughter. And hark ye, my pet! Thou hast a fair outside, and a pretty wit enough of thine own. Yea, a pretty wit enough! Thou wilt think better of it when thou hast seen more of other people's wits. Now, with thy outside and thy inside, thou art the very man to win a young girl's heart. Never doubt it! I tell thee it shall be so. Put but a bold face on the matter, sigh, smile, flourish thy hat, thrust forth thy leg like a dancing-master, put thy right hand to the left side of thy waistcoat, and pretty Polly Gookin is thine own!"

All this while the new creature had been sucking in and exhaling the vapory fragrance of his pipe, and seemed now to continue this occupation as much for the enjoyment it afforded as because it was an essential condition of his existence. It was wonderful to see how exceedingly like a human being it behaved. Its eyes (for it appeared to possess a pair) were bent on Mother Rigby, and at suitable junctures it nodded or shook its head. Neither did it lack words proper for the occasion: "Really! Indeed! Pray tell me! Is it possible! Upon my word! By no means! Oh! Ah! Hem!" and other such weighty utterances as imply attention, inquiry, acquiescence, or dissent on the part of the auditor. Even had you stood by and seen the scarecrow made, you could scarcely have resisted the conviction that it perfectly understood the cunning counsels which the old witch poured into its counterfeit of an ear. The more earnestly it applied its lips to the pipe, the more distinctly was its human likeness stamped among visible realities, the more sagacious grew its expression, the more lifelike its gestures and movements, and the more intelligibly audible its voice. Its garments, too, glistened so much the brighter with an illusory magnificence. The very pipe, in which burned the spell of all this wonderwork, ceased to appear as a smoke-blackened earthen stump, and became a meerschaum, with painted bowl and amber mouthpiece.

It might be apprehended, however, that as the life of the illusion seemed identical with the vapor of the pipe, it would terminate simultaneously with the reduction of the tobacco to ashes. But the beldam foresaw the difficulty.

"Hold thou the pipe, my precious one," said she, "while I fill it for thee again."

It was sorrowful to behold how the fine gentleman began to fade back into a scarecrow while Mother Rigby shook the ashes out of the pipe and proceeded to replenish it from her tobacco-box.

"Dickon," cried she, in her high, sharp tone, "another coal for this pipe!"

No sooner said than the intensely red speck of fire was glowing

within the pipe-bowl; and the scarecrow, without waiting for the witch's bidding, applied the tube to his lips and drew in a few short, convulsive whiffs, which soon, however, became regular and equable.

"Now, mine own heart's darling," quoth Mother Rigby, "whatever may happen to thee, thou must stick to thy pipe. Thy life is in it; and that, at least, thou knowest well, if thou knowest nought besides. Stick to thy pipe, I say! Smoke, puff, blow thy cloud; and tell the people, if any question be made, that it is for thy health, and that so the physician orders thee to do. And, sweet one, when thou shalt find thy pipe getting low, go apart into some corner, and (first filling thyself with smoke) cry sharply, 'Dickon, a fresh pipe of tobacco!' and, 'Dickon, another coal for my pipe!' and have it into thy pretty mouth as speedily as may be. Else, instead of a gallant gentleman in a gold-laced coat, thou wilt be but a jumble of sticks and tattered clothes, and a bag of straw, and a withered pumpkin! Now depart, my treasure, and good luck go with thee!"

"Never fear, mother!" said the figure, in a stout voice, and sending forth a courageous whiff of smoke, "I will thrive, if an honest man and a gentleman may!"

"Oh, thou wilt be the death of me!" cried the old witch, convulsed with laughter. "That was well said. If an honest man and a gentleman may! Thou playest thy part to perfection. Get along with thee for a smart fellow; and I will wager on thy head, as a man of pith and substance, with a brain and what they call a heart, and all else that a man should have, against any other thing on two legs. I hold myself a better witch than yesterday, for thy sake. Did not I make thee? And I defy any witch in New England to make such another! Here, take my staff along with thee!"

The staff, though it was but a plain oaken stick, immediately took the aspect of a gold-headed cane.

"That gold head has as much sense in it as thine own," said Mother Rigby, "and it will guide thee straight to worshipful Master Gookin's door. Get thee gone, my pretty pet, my darling, my precious one, my treasure; and if any ask thy name, it is Feathertop. For thou hast a feather in thy hat, and I have thrust a handful of feathers into the hollow of thy head, and thy wig, too, is of the fashion they call Feathertop — so be Feathertop thy name!"

And, issuing from the cottage, Feathertop strode manfully toward town. Mother Rigby stood at the threshold, well pleased to see how the sunbeams glistened on him, as if all his magnificence were real, and how diligently and lovingly he smoked his pipe, and how handsomely he walked, in spite of a little stiffness of his legs. She watched him until out of sight, and threw a witch benediction after her darling, when a turn of the road snatched him from her view.

Betimes in the forenoon, when the principal street of the neighboring town was just at its acme of life and bustle, a stranger of very distinguished figure was seen on the sidewalk. His port as well as his garments betokened nothing short of nobility. He wore a richly embroidered plum-colored coat, a waistcoat of costly velvet, magnificently adorned with golden foliage, a pair of splendid scarlet breeches, and the finest and glossiest of white silk stockings. His head was covered with a peruke, so daintily powdered and adjusted that it would have been sacrilege to disorder it with a hat; which, therefore (and it was a gold-laced hat, set off with a snowy feather), he carried beneath his arm. On the breast of his coat glistened a star. He managed his gold-headed cane with an airy grace, peculiar to the fine gentlemen of the period; and, to give the highest possible finish to his equipment, he had lace ruffles at his wrist, of a most ethereal delicacy, sufficiently avouching how idle and aristocratic must be the hands which they half concealed.

It was a remarkable point in the accoutrement of this brilliant personage that he held in his left hand a fantastic kind of a pipe, with an exquisitely painted bowl and an amber mouthpiece. This he applied to his lips as often as every five or six paces, and inhaled a deep whiff of smoke, which, after being retained a moment in his lungs, might be seen to eddy gracefully from his mouth and nostrils.

As may well be supposed, the street was all astir to find out the stranger's name.

"It is some great nobleman, beyond question," said one of the towns-people. "Do you see the star at his breast?"

"Nay; it is too bright to be seen," said another. "Yes; he must needs be a nobleman, as you say. But by what conveyance, think you, can his lord ship have voyaged or traveled hither? There has been no vessel from the old country for a month past; and if he has arrived overland from the southward, pray where are his attendants and equipage?"

"He needs no equipage to set off his rank," remarked a third. "If he came among us in rags, nobility would shine through a hole in his elbow. I never saw such dignity of aspect. He has the old Norman blood in his veins, I warrant him."

"I rather take him to be a Dutchman, or one of your high Germans," said another citizen. "The men of those countries have always the pipe at their mouths."

"And so has a Turk," answered his companion. "But, in my judgment, this stranger hath been bred at the French court, and hath there learned politeness and grace of manner, which none understand so well as the nobility of France. That gait, now! A vulgar spectator might deem it stiff — he might call it a hitch and jerk — but, to my eye, it hath an unspeakable majesty, and must have been acquired by constant observation of the deportment of the Grand Monarque. The stranger's character and office are evident enough. He is a French ambassador, come to treat with our rulers about the cession of Canada."

"More probably a Spaniard," said another, "and hence his yellow complexion. Or, most likely, he is from the Havana, or from some port on the Spanish Main, and comes to make investigation about the piracies which our Governor is thought to connive at. Those settlers in Peru and Mexico have skins as yellow as the gold which they dig out of their mines."

"Yellow or not," cried a lady, "he is a beautiful man! — so tall, so slender! such a fine, noble face, with so well-shaped a nose, and all that delicacy of expression about the mouth! And, bless me, how bright his star is! It positively shoots out flames!"

"So do your eyes, fair lady," said the stranger, with a bow and a flourish of his pipe; for he was just passing at the instant. "Upon my honor, they have quite dazzled me."

"Was ever so original and exquisite a compliment?" murmured the lady, in an ecstasy of delight.

Amid the general admiration excited by the stranger's appearance, there were only two dissenting voices. One was that of an impertinent cur, which, after snuffing at the heels of the glistening figure, put its tail between its legs and skulked into its master's back yard, vociferating an execrable howl. The other dissentient was a young child, who squalled at the fullest stretch of his lungs, and babbled some unintelligible nonsense about a pumpkin.

Feathertop, meanwhile, pursued his way along the street. Except for the few complimentary words to the lady, and now and then a slight inclination of the head in requital of the profound reverences of the bystanders, he seemed wholly absorbed in his pipe. There needed no other proof of his rank and consequence than the perfect equanimity with which he comported himself, while the curiosity and admiration of the town swelled almost into clamor around him. With a crowd gathering behind his footsteps, he finally reached the mansion-house of the worshipful Justice Gookin, entered the gate, ascended the steps of the front door, and knocked. In the interim, before his summons was answered, the stranger was observed to shake the ashes out of his pipe.

"What did he say in that sharp voice?" inquired one of the spectators.

"Nay, I know not," answered his friend. "But the sun dazzles my eyes strangely. How dim and faded his lordship looks all of a sudden! Bless my wits, what is the matter with me?"

"The wonder is," said the other, "that his pipe, which was out only an instant ago, should be all alight again, and with the reddest coal I ever saw! There is something mysterious about this stranger. What a whiff of smoke was that! Dim and faded did you call him? Why, as he turns about the star on his breast is all ablaze."

"It is, indeed," said his companion; "and it will go near to dazzle pretty Polly Gookin, whom I see peeping at it out of the chamber window."

The door being now opened, Feathertop turned to the crowd, made a stately bend of his body like a great man acknowledging the reverence of the meaner sort, and vanished into the house. There was a mysterious kind of a smile, if it might not better be called a grin or grimace, upon his visage; but, of all the throng that beheld him, not an individual appears to have possessed insight enough to detect the illusive character of the stranger except a little child and a cur dog.

Our legend here loses somewhat of its continuity, and, passing over the preliminary explanation between Feathertop and the merchant, goes in quest of the pretty Polly Gookin. She was a damsel of a soft, round figure, with light hair and blue eyes, and a fair, rosy face, which seemed neither very shrewd nor very simple. This young lady had caught a glimpse of the glistening stranger while standing at the threshold, and had forthwith put on a laced cap, a string of beads, her finest kerchief, and her stiffest damask petticoat in preparation for the interview. Hurrying from her chamber to the parlor, she had ever since been view-ing herself in the large looking-glass and practicing pretty airs — now a smile, now a ceremonious dignity of aspect, and now a softer smile than the former, kissing her hand likewise, tossing her head, and managing her fan; while within the mirror an unsubstantial little maid repeated every gesture and did all the foolish things that Polly did, but without making her ashamed of them. In short, it was the fault of pretty Polly's ability, rather than her will, if she failed to be as complete an artifice as the illustrious Feathertop himself; and, when she thus tampered with her own simplicity, the witch's phantom might well hope to win her.

No sooner did Polly hear her father's gouty footsteps approaching the parlor door, accompanied with the stiff clatter of Feathertop's high-heeled shoes, than she seated herself bolt upright and innocently began warbling a song.

"Polly! daughter Polly!" cried the old merchant. "Come hither, child."

Master Gookin's aspect, as he opened the door, was doubtful and troubled.

"This gentleman," continued he, presenting the stranger, "is the Chevalier Feathertop — nay, I beg his pardon, my lord Feathertop — who hath brought me a token of remembrance from an ancient friend of mine. Pay your duty to his lordship, child, and honor him as his quality deserves."

After these few words of introduction, the worshipful magistrate immediately quitted the room. But, even in that brief moment, had the fair Polly glanced aside at her father instead of devoting herself wholly to the brilliant guest, she might have taken warning of some mischief nigh at hand. The old man was nervous, fidgety, and very pale. Purposing a smile of courtesy, he had deformed his face with a sort of galvanic grin, which, when Feathertop's back was turned, he exchanged for a scowl, at the same time shaking his fist and stamping his gouty foot — an incivility which brought its retribution along with it. The truth appears to have been that Mother Rigby's word of introduction, what-ever it might be, had operated far more on the rich merchant's fears than on his good will. Moreover, being a man of wonderfully acute observation, he had noticed that these painted figures on the bowl of Feathertop's pipe were in motion. Looking more closely, he became convinced that these figures were a party of little demons, each duly provided with horns and a tail, and dancing hand in hand, with gestures of diabolical merriment, round the circumference of the pipe bowl. As if to confirm his suspicions, while Master Gookin ushered his guest along a dusky passage from his private room to the parlor, the star on Feathertop's breast had scintillated actual flames and threw a flickering gleam upon the wall, the ceiling, and the floor.

With such sinister prognostics manifesting themselves on all hands, it is not to be marveled at that the merchant should have felt that he was committing his daughter to a very questionable acquaintance. He cursed, in his secret soul, the insinuating elegance of Feathertop's manners, as this brilliant personage bowed, smiled, put his hand on his heart, inhaled a long whiff from his pipe, and enriched the atmosphere with the smoky vapor of a fragrant and visible sigh. Gladly would poor Master Gookin have thrust his dangerous guest into the street; but there was a constraint and terror within him. This respectable old gentleman, we fear, at an earlier period of life, had given some pledge or other to the evil principle, and perhaps was now to redeem it by the sacrifice of his daughter.

It so happened that the parlor door was partly of glass, shaded by a silken curtain, the folds of which hung a little awry. So strong was the merchant's interest in witnessing what was to ensue between the fair Polly and the gallant Feathertop that, after quitting the room, he could by no means refrain from peeping through the crevice of the curtain.

But there was nothing very miraculous to be seen; nothing — except the trifles previously noticed — to confirm the idea of a supernatural peril environing the pretty Polly. The stranger, it is true, was evidently a thorough and practised man of the world, systematic and self-possessed, and therefore the sort of a person to whom a parent ought not to confide a simple, young girl without due watchfulness for the result. The worthy magistrate, who had been conversant with all degrees and qualities of mankind, could not but perceive every motion and gesture of the distinguished Feathertop came in its proper place; nothing had been left rude or native in him; a well-digested conventionalism had incorporated itself thoroughly with his substance and transformed him into a work of art. Perhaps it was this peculiarity that invested him with a species of ghastliness and awe. It is the effect of anything completely and consummately artificial, in human shape, that the person impresses us as an unreality and as having hardly pith enough to cast a shadow upon the floor. As regarded Feathertop, all this resulted in a wild, extravagant, and fantastical impression, as if his life and being were akin to the smoke that curled upward from his pipe.

But pretty Polly Gookin felt not thus. The pair were now promenading the room: Feathertop with his dainty stride and no less dainty grimace; the girl with a native maidenly grace, just touched, not spoiled, by a slightly affected manner, which seemed caught from the perfect artifice of her companion. The longer the interview continued, the more charmed was pretty Polly, until, within the first quarter of an hour (as the old magistrate noted by his watch), she was evidently beginning to be in love. Nor need it have been witchcraft that subdued her in such a hurry; the poor child's heart, it may be, was so very fervent that it melted her with its own warmth as reflected from the hollow semblance of a lover. No matter what Feathertop said, his words found depth and reverberation in her ear; no matter what he did, his action was heroic to her eye. And, by this time, it is to be supposed there was a blush on Polly's cheek, a tender smile about her mouth, and a liquid softness in her glance; while the star kept coruscating on Feathertop's breast, and the little demons careered with more frantic merriment than ever about the circumference of his pipe bowl. Oh, pretty Polly Gookin, why should these imps rejoice so madly that a silly maiden's heart was about to be given to a shadow! Is it so unusual a misfortune, so rare a triumph?

By and by Feathertop paused, and throwing himself into an imposing attitude, seemed to summon the fair girl to survey his figure and resist him longer if she could. His star, his embroidery, his buckles, glowed at that instant with unutterable splendor; the picturesque hues of his attire took a richer depth of coloring; there was a gleam and polish over his

whole presence betokening the perfect witchery of well-ordered manners. The maiden raised her eyes and suffered them to linger upon her companion with a bashful and admiring gaze. Then, as if desirous of judging what value her own simple comeliness might have side by side with so much brilliancy, she cast a glance toward the full-length looking-glass in front of which they happened to be standing. It was one of the truest plates in the world and incapable of flattery. No sooner did the images therein reflected meet Polly's eye than she shrieked, shrank from the stranger's side, gazed at him for a moment in the wildest dismay, and sank insensible upon the floor. Feathertop, likewise, had looked toward the mirror, and there beheld, not the glittering mockery of his outside show, but a picture of the sordid patchwork of his real composition, stripped of all witchcraft.

The wretched simulacrum! We almost pity him. He threw up his arms, with an expression of despair, that went further than any of his previous manifestations toward vindicating his claims to be reckoned human. For perchance the only time, since this so often empty and deceptive life of mortals began its course, an illusion had seen and fully recognized itself.

Mother Rigby was seated by her kitchen hearth in the twilight of this eventful day, and had just shaken the ashes out of a new pipe, when she heard a hurried tramp along the road. Yet it did not seem so much the tramp of human footsteps as the clatter of sticks or the rattling of dry bones.

"Ha!" thought the old witch, "what step is that? Whose skeleton is out of its grave now, I wonder?"

A figure burst headlong into the cottage door. It was Feathertop! His pipe was still alight; the star still flamed upon his breast; the embroidery still glowed upon his garments, nor had he lost, in any degree or manner that could be estimated, the aspect that assimilated him with our mortal brotherhood. But yet, in some indescribable way (as is the case with all that has deluded us when once found out), the poor reality was felt beneath the cunning artifice.

"What has gone wrong?" demanded the witch. "Did yonder sniffling hypocrite thrust my darling from his door? The villain! I'll set twenty fiends to torment him till he offer thee his daughter on his bended knees!"

"No, mother," said Feathertop despondingly, "it was not that."

"Did the girl scorn my precious one?" asked Mother Rigby, her fierce eyes glowing like two coals of Tophet. "I'll cover her face with pimples! Her nose shall be as red as the coal in thy pipe! Her front teeth shall drop out! In a week hence she shall not be worth thy having!"

"Let her alone, mother," answered poor Feathertop. "The girl was half won; and methinks a kiss from her sweet lips might have made me altogether human. But," he added, after a brief pause and then a howl of self-contempt, "I've seen myself, mother! I've seen myself for the wretched, ragged, empty thing I am! I'll exist no longer!"

Snatching the pipe from his mouth, he flung it with all his might against the chimney, and at the same instant sank upon the floor, a medley of straw and tattered garments, with some sticks protruding from the heap, and a shriveled pumpkin in the midst. The eyeholes were now lusterless; but the rudely carved gap, that just before had been a mouth, still seemed to twist itself into a despairing grin, and was so far human.

"Poor fellow!" quoth Mother Rigby, with a rueful glance at the relics of her ill-fated contrivance. "My poor, dear, pretty Feathertop! There are thousands upon thousands of coxcombs and charlatans in the world, made up of just such a jumble of worn-out, forgotten, and good-for-nothing trash as he was! Yet they live in fair repute, and never see themselves for what they are. And why should my poor puppet be the only one to know himself, and perish for it?"

While thus muttering, the witch had filled a fresh pipe of tobacco, and held the stem between her fingers, as doubtful whether to thrust it into her own mouth or Feathertop's.

"Poor Feathertop!" she continued. "I could easily give him another chance and send him forth again tomorrow. But, no! His feelings are too tender, his sensibilities too deep. He seems to have too much heart to bustle for his own advantage in such an empty and heartless world. Well, well! I'll make a scarecrow of him after all. 'Tis an innocent and useful vocation, and will suit my darling well; and, if each of his human brethren had as fit a one, 'twould be the better for mankind; and as for this pipe of tobacco, I need it more than he."

So saying, Mother Rigby put the stem between her lips. "Dickon!" cried she, in her high, sharp tone, "Another coal for my pipe!"

THE RICH MAN'S PLACE

HORACE E. SCUDDER

*Horace Elisha Scudder (1838–1902) was a Bostonian man of letters, and in his later years was editor of the **Atlantic Monthly**. Today he is best remembered as the editor of the **Riverside Magazine for Young People** (1867–70), a forerunner of **St. Nicholas**. The most distinctive feature of the **Riverside Magazine** was its inclusion of ten new tales by Hans Christian Andersen, in Scudder's sympathetic translation; some of them had not yet appeared even in Danish. Scudder's friendship with the elderly Andersen is documented in **The Andersen-Scudder Letters** (ed. Westergaard, 1949). Scudder frankly admitted that his own children's stories were modeled on Andersen's, but he understood that, for America, mere imitation of European tales would not suffice. He wrote to Andersen, "It is our effort to adapt the magazine to the wants of children in a new country, where European civilization is found, modified by the circumstances of nature and government." "The Rich Man's Place" was first published in **Dream Children** (1864); Scudder's other collections for children include **Seven Little People and Their Friends** (1862) and **Stories from My Attic** (1869).*

THE RICH man had a splendid place — a house and barns, and a great pleasure park — but it was long since he had seen his place, for he had been traveling abroad. When people travel abroad, they expect to learn much, and the rich man when he came home had no doubt learned a great many things. He had brought away as much of other countries as he could carry — a little in his head, but a good deal in boxes. When these were unpacked, there came forth pictures and statuary and malachite tables, and at least three cart-loads of curious things, which he arranged about the house, so that when his friends came to see him, they all said it was nearly as well as visiting foreign lands themselves; for when they entered the house, the rich man would remind them where he had been. "This hat-tree," he would say, as they took off their hats, "is made of wood from the Black Forest," and then they would shut their eyes, and fancy themselves there. "This table on which I keep my clothes-brush," he would continue, "is a malachite table from Russia." And then they would ask him if he saw the Czar. When they entered the parlor, he would take them on a tour about the room, and feed their imagination with a stone from the field of Waterloo, a splinter from John Knox's house, a piece of pottery from Herculaneum, and a scimitar from Greece; and, if left to themselves, they were given a book of views, or a stereoscope, or allowed to stand before the *étagère*, and handle the Swiss toys and Scotch pebbles. Oh, it was precisely the same as going abroad, and so the guests all said.

But it was best when someone came who had also traveled, and perhaps with the rich man himself; then the guests would listen as one said to the other, "Do you remember that night on the Campagna?"

And the other would say, "Ah, indeed!" and look knowing. "But the Carnival, ah!" he would rejoin, and turn round to the guests, humming the "Carnival of Venice."

"What a tame country ours is!" the guests would sigh to themselves.

Now the rich man walked over his place when he had unpacked his curiosities. His father and grandfather had lived there before him, and the trees were old and large. It was certainly a noble plantation, but it did not please the rich man. It had had its own way too much, something was wanting — he had been abroad, and seen parks — what was it?

"This place needs attention," said he, "and I am determined to improve it." So he bought statues, and placed them about the grounds — plaster statues of young men leaning on hoes, and young girls with aprons full of flowers, and in a basin he set up a statue of Venus rising out of the sea foam. It was an extraordinary thing; a water-pipe ran round the base, and little jets threw out spurts of water which were to cover Venus, and look like a veil. But he did not succeed very well with this, and people found considerable fault with it. He built stone terraces, and ran straight gravel walks so wide that ten could walk abreast, and so long that one could prove the earth was round by watching a man appear at the other end. The cedar-trees he had cut after his own taste, and of these he was very proud. The gardener, with a pair of shears, clipped the branches according to certain models. One tree looked like a bear, another like a lion, a third like a giraffe, and in the middle stood one which was precisely like a man.

"Now this is like something," said the rich man, admiring it; "still something is lacking. Ah! I know, it is a fountain." So he had a fountain made, and cut down the trees around it, that he might have a view of it from the house. It had almost as many jets as there were days in the year, one never could tell how it would look next.

"I believe I have everything after my mind now," said he, "and I will give a fête to all my neighbors. The poor people, too, shall be allowed to come in and stay at a distance. They will make the scene picturesque." He gave out word of the fête, and you may be sure everybody was delighted to come, for his grounds had been kept shut, and it was said that wonderful improvements had been made.

The day was spent in all manner of gaiety. People walked over the place, and admired the cedar lion, and bear, and giraffe, and colossal man, and, most of all, the fountain which changed its form every five minutes. In the pond beneath swam beautiful swans, while gazelles fled timidly about, and storks stood, as usual, like soldiers who had come back from the war with one leg. It would be impossible to repeat what everybody said and thought.

The evening was even finer. There were fireworks, Chinese lanterns, and fire-balloons, the fountain playing all the time. The guests were well placed, a band of music played for them, and the poor people were in the distance. Everyone was delighted. Rockets, and Roman candles, and pin-wheels, and pigeons followed so rapidly, and were so brilliant, that people got tired of saying "Oh!" The last piece was the most magnificent. It was a battle-piece. Six frigates appeared, and fired fireworks at each other; the cannon boomed, the rockets went off in every direction, and at last the ships all burned up together, and after a great explosion, and red, green, and blue lights, everything went out, and it was as black as it could be. The fountain, too, stopped, and the day was over.

It was soon perfectly still also; for as soon as the fireworks ceased, everyone left the grounds. Yet a few remained; there was life there yet. Two hens, who had each sat up to see the fireworks, came upon one another as they were going by different ways to the barn-yard. One was black, the other was yellow, and so we will distinguish them, for otherwise they had no names.

"What! You here?" exclaimed Black, who naturally saw the other first. "This is rather late to be out."

"The same to you," rejoined Yellow. "For my part I rather enjoy this fine night, though it certainly is somewhat dark. I had no idea that night was quite so black."

"But it was bright enough just now," said the other. "That was a fine show!"

"Very!" said Yellow; "But, neighbor, let us not stand here. If you are on your way to the house, as I presume you are, let us go in company." So they walked on together, much to the relief of each.

"Yes, it was a superb show," resumed Yellow; "something unusual. I never saw anything so magnificent. John came into the house one night with two lanterns to look for eggs, and almost blinded us, but that was nothing to this."

"I suppose all the world was there," said Black; "I didn't count, but made a rough guess. No one would miss such a sight. It probably only happens once."

"Yes," said Yellow, "it is precisely like our golden egg," — and she sighed — "once, and only once. The rich man has done it, and the world may now stop."

"I suppose there could be nothing grander done," observed Black.

"You may be sure of that. It was no common thing. We go on laying eggs every day, but they are nothing but shell eggs. The rich man has been round the globe, and when he comes home you don't think he would settle down like people, and just mind his business! That would be laying shell eggs only. No, he lays the golden egg, depend upon it." The yellow hen, who prided herself on her wisdom, would have gone on much longer upon the subject of eggs, but at this moment there was a rustling in the bushes.

"The fire-sticks are all down, I hope," whispered Black. "I dodged about when they fell before"; but as she spoke, the Stork stepped in a dignified manner on to the gravel-walk, and approached them.

"Good evening," said Yellow, in a faint voice, and Black tried to say the same; the Stork took no notice of them, but Yellow, seeing more distinctly who it was, and being anxious to talk, stopped her walk, and continued, "I was just saying to my friend how fine it was tonight. We are fortunate in living in such times. Nothing like it ever known before. The golden egg, no doubt, for I have a theory, friend, that hens are not the only ones that are trying to lay golden eggs." The yellow hen always came round to this point, and would have now come round to it again, but the Stork interrupted her.

"When you have seen as much of the world as I have, you will change your mind. Eggs!" and the Stork drew himself up on one leg; "Eggs! there is something better to be done. The rich man is a fool. Let him stand on one leg and think, instead of burning his fingers with matches. To find out what we are made of and what is to come of it — that is the only thing," and he walked away.

"Just hear him!" said Black. "Suppose we see what we are made of. But I can't understand. Can you?"

"Yes, but it's not easy to explain," said Yellow, and they talked no more. Yet they listened, for they were passing through the cedar-trees, and conversation was there going on.

"Say what you will," said the colossal man, "it is very fine to look like a man."

It was to an elm that he spoke, and the elm replied, "Methinks you have lost your good sense, friend, since the gardener trimmed you. You were very contented then, and had no foolish thoughts."

"Foolish thoughts! I think of the fireworks, and the fountain, and the music, as the rich man does. Don't speak of those old days when I was in low society."

"Is this anything like a roar?" said the cedar lion, rubbing his branches. "I think I made a pretty good lion."

"In time! in time!" said the cedar bear. "I believe my business is to growl — what do you say to this?" and he growled as he thought.

"It is extraordinary how tall I am," said the cedar giraffe. "This is living to some purpose. I really never knew before what I could be."

"Just hear them all!" said the elm to a neighbor. "I thought they would have been too ashamed to speak, and yet they now despise us. We are only trees, they tell us. Well, I am content. It is good enough for me. Here I have grown, and what I shall come to I can't say, but something fine, no doubt. So, neighbor, I think the best we can do is to grow."

"How will that do?" asked the black hen.

"I think we had best keep on laying eggs," said Yellow. "Perhaps the golden one will turn up after all; who knows?" and they walked on to the barn, where they had to stay outside till morning.

The trees now were also silent, for steps were heard. Two friends, an artist and a poet, out of the crowd of guests, were walking past, enjoying the quiet. They walked to another part of the grounds, away from the still fountain, and the tortured trees, and the blackened fireworks.

"Here are trees one might paint," said the artist, looking round with admiration upon some oaks. "Those cedars! Good for firewood. But an oak looks well in a picture. By the way, that would have been a fine night-scene to paint — the fireworks lighting up the crowd of poor people on the grass — a pretty scene; it had good points."

"The heavens make the most splendid display of fire," said the poet, looking up. "Let us walk here all night, and watch the changes of the sky and see how we are affected — what thoughts we have, and then I can put it down in verse." Then they talked of nature and art, and unity, and the poetic soul, but no one wants to listen to such talk. Indeed, they tired of it soon, and passed out of the gate, somewhat sleepy. It was the gate out of which the poor people went: but all had not gone.

Under the trees still walked two of these. They also had seen the fireworks, and they had seen the trees and the stars. But they had better things to talk of.

"I would not exchange all this for you," said he.

"Well," said she, "if it were yours I do not think I should love you more."

WHAT THEY DID NOT DO ON THE BIRTHDAY OF JACOB ABBOTT B., FAMILIARLY CALLED SNIBBUGGLEDYBOOZLEDOM

M. S. B.

❧ *I have not been able to discover the identity of M. S. B., the author of this joyful skit on the gentle realism of popular children's author Jacob Abbott. Indeed this story, published in the illustrious children's magazine* St. Nicholas *in January 1876, with scratchy illustrations by J. B., is the only piece of writing I can attribute to her, or him. Yet its tongue-in-cheek logic, celebrating the strangeness of the ordinary world, clearly paves the way for Carl Sandburg's* Rootabaga Stories; *there is the same sense of verve, panache, and shared fun between parent and child. A more recent comparison might be the English poet Adrian Mitchell's "Nothingmas Day": "It was Nothingmas Eve and all the children in Notown were not tingling with excitement as they lay unawake in their heaps." Nonsense writing, often regarded as a specifically British skill, is here given a rambunctious, wisecracking American expression. This is the first, but not the last story in this book to have appeared in* St. Nicholas. *The magazine was first issued in 1873 by* Scribner's Monthly, *who had in 1871 absorbed the* Riverside Magazine, *and in 1874 also acquired* Our Young Folks. *From 1873 until 1905, its glory years, it was edited by Mary Mapes Dodge, who persuaded the best writers of the day to contribute, while also encouraging unknowns. To browse through a run of* St. Nicholas *is to constantly encounter both classic tales in their freshest bloom, and a wealth of forgotten gems, such as this off-the-wall birthday tribute to Jacob Abbott B., familiarly called Snibbuggledyboozledom.* ❧

I WONDER if anybody in this city remembered that last Wednesday was Snibbuggledyboozledom's birthday. I guess nobody thought a word about it until the next day, which was a great pity, for everybody ought to have remembered it and turned out, and shouted and fired guns, and made speeches and processions; and I would write and tell you all about what they did. But as they didn't celebrate the day at all, I can only write what they *didn't* do.

In the first place then, we were not waked up before light by a crowd of three or four hundred boys shouting and firing guns and firecrackers and parlor-match pistols, and yelling, "Hurrah for Abbott, seven years old!" "Three cheers for Jakey, seven years old!" Then at sunrise the big bell in the fire-tower did not strike seven times: "Boo-oong! Boo-oong! Boo-oong! Boo-oong! Boo-oong! Boo-oong! Boo-oong!" and all the other bells in the steeples didn't strike in with a tremendous uproar: "Ding-dong-ding! Ding-dong-ding! Ding-dong-ding!" just as loud as they ever couldn't sound. What a clatter they didn't make!

And all the flags in the city were not flying all day from sunrise till dark. And the boys all over the city didn't keep at work every minute of the day popping off fire-crackers and torpedoes, and little toy cannon that would shoot off a shot about as big as this: ● and used a nail for a ramrod. Sometimes they wouldn't light the crackers and throw them up

in the air, to see them go off before they came down again; and sometimes they wouldn't hold them out in little iron pistols, to look like
shooting; and sometimes they wouldn't bury them in the ground, and
then touch them off, so as to throw the dirt up all around like a mine;
and sometimes they wouldn't put a fire-cracker on a little chip (for a
boat) and sail it off on the water, and light the cracker to see it blow up
the boat. I tell you they didn't have a *splendid* time, and every boy's father
didn't give him ten cents, all for his own, to buy peanuts or candy, or
anything else he wanted.

And then in the afternoon there wasn't a grand procession three
miles long, with lots of soldiers in bright-colored uniforms, and brass
bands, each one with a drum-major with a tall bearskin cap and a gold-
headed staff, and Masons with queer little white aprons, and firemen
with their engines and hose-carts and ladder-trucks, and the mayor and
common council, and three trained monkeys on as many little ponies,
and an elephant and two camels, and a clumsy rhinoceros with his horn
on his nose (a very ugly nose too), and thirteen ministers in carriages.
And they didn't go through all the streets and up to the park, and then
the mayor didn't make a grand speech two hours long, telling how
gratified he wasn't to assist in the celebration of such a day, and what an
honor he didn't consider it to the city to be the residence of two such
great folks as himself and Snibbuggledyboozledom.

And then they didn't have a grand display of fireworks — great rockets that went s-s-s-izz away up in the air and then sent down lots of red
and purple and green stars, and wheels that spun around and around
with a whiz-z-z and threw off all manner of beautiful sparks, and Roman
candles that burned with sparks and threw up with a pop brilliant

white and colored balls. And at the end they didn't send up an enormous fire-balloon, thirty-five feet across, with red and white and blue stripes up and down it, and "Snibbuggledyboozledom, 1875," in large gold letters reaching all around it. And it didn't sail, sail, sail away, shining at first like a great big moon, and sailing, sailing, sailing further off till it looked no bigger than a star, and then sailing, sailing, sailing away till we couldn't see it at all. And I don't believe it ever came down at all, anywhere. Because, you see, if it didn't ever go up, it couldn't ever come down!

And that was the end of the things that didn't happen on the boy's birthday. Only the next day the papers didn't have lots of news about it — how one man didn't have his hat knocked off by a rocket that went along straight instead of going up in the air, and fifteen boys and three girls didn't get their fingers and faces burned with the fire-crackers and things, and ten horses were not frightened and didn't run away, smashing nine wagons and barking fifteen trees, and five houses were not set on fire by sparks and crackers, and the usual number of such mishaps did not take place. And there were not about fifteen thousand pints of peanuts sold, and five thousand glasses of soda water, and a corresponding amount of other good things.

And then (this part did really happen) everybody went to bed and to sleep, just as if it had been any common day.

THE BEE-MAN OF ORN

FRANK STOCKTON

➜ Frank Richard Stockton (1834–1902) was born in Philadelphia. He recalled, "I was very young when I determined to write some fairy tales because my mind was full of them." But, in a very American spirit, he wanted the characters of his fairyland to act "as far as possible for them to do so, as if they were inhabitants of the real world." This tension in Stockton's tales between fantasy and reality predates the similar attempt of L. Frank Baum to write "modern tales about modern fairies." Stockton's early fairy tales appeared in the **Riverside Magazine,** *and many of the later ones in* **St. Nicholas,** *of which he was assistant editor from 1874 until 1878. "The Bee-man of Orn" first appeared as "The Bee-man and His Original Form" in* **St. Nicholas** *November 1883; the text here is the slightly revised version from* **The Bee-man of Orn and Other Fanciful Tales** *(1887). Stockton's other books of fairy tales include* **The Floating Prince and Other Fairy Tales** *(1881) and* **Ting-a-ling Tales** *(1901); he is also remembered for an adult short story, "The Lady or the Tiger?" ⬅*

IN THE ancient country of Orn there lived an old man who was called the Bee-man, because his whole time was spent in the company of bees. He lived in a small hut, which was nothing more than an immense bee-hive, for these little creatures had built their honeycombs in every corner of the one room it contained — on the shelves, under the little table, all about the rough bench on which the old man sat, and even about the headboard and along the sides of his low bed. All day the air of the room was thick with buzzing insects, but this did not interfere in any way with the old Bee-man, who walked in among them, ate his meals, and went to sleep without the slightest fear of being stung. He had lived with the bees so long, they had become so accustomed to him, and his skin was so tough and hard, that they no more thought of stinging him than they would of stinging a tree or a stone.

A swarm of bees made their hive in a pocket of his old leather doublet; and when he put on this coat to take one of his long walks in the forest in search of wild bees' nests, he was very glad to have this hive with him, for if he did not find any wild honey, he would put his hand in his pocket and take out a piece of honeycomb for a luncheon. The bees in his pocket worked very industriously, and he was always certain of having something to eat with him wherever he went. He lived principally upon honey; and when he needed bread or meat, he carried some fine combs to a village nearby and bartered them for other food.

He was ugly, untidy, shriveled, and sun-burnt. He was poor, and the bees seemed to be his only friends. But, for all that, he was happy and contented. He had all the honey he wanted, and his bees, whom he considered the best company in the world, were as friendly and sociable as they could be, and seemed to increase in number every day.

One day there stopped at the hut of the Bee-man a Junior Sorcerer. This young person, who was a student of magic, necromancy, and the kindred arts, was much interested in the Bee-man, whom he had frequently noticed in his wanderings, and he considered him an admirable subject for study. He had had a great deal of useful practice in endeavoring to find out, by the various rules and laws of sorcery, exactly why the old Bee-man did not happen to be something that he was not, and why he was what he happened to be. He had studied this matter a long time, and had found out something.

"Do you know," he said, when the Bee-man came out of his hut, "that you have been transformed?"

"What do you mean by that?" said the other, much surprised.

"You have surely heard of animals and human beings who have been magically transformed into different kinds of creatures?"

"Yes, I have heard of these things," said the Bee-man. "But what have I been transformed from?"

"That is more than I know," said the Junior Sorcerer. "But one thing is certain — you ought to be changed back. If you will find out what you have been transformed from, I will see that you are made all right again. Nothing would please me better than to attend to such a case."

Then, having a great many things to study and investigate, the Junior Sorcerer went his way.

This information greatly disturbed the mind of the Bee-man. If he had been changed from something else, he ought to be that other thing, whatever it was. He ran after the young man, and overtook him.

"If you know, kind sir," he said, "that I have been transformed, you surely are able to tell me what it is that I was."

"No," said the Junior Sorcerer, "my studies have not proceeded far enough for that. When I become a senior I can tell you all about it. But, in the meantime, it will be well for you to try to discover for yourself your original form, and when you have done that, I will get some of the learned masters of my art to restore you to it. It will be easy enough to do that, but you cannot expect them to take the time and trouble to find out what it was."

With these words, he hurried away, and was soon lost to view.

Greatly disquieted, the Bee-man retraced his steps, and went to his hut. Never before had he heard anything which had so troubled him.

"I wonder what I was transformed from?" he thought, seating himself on his rough bench. "Could it have been a giant, or a powerful prince, or some gorgeous being whom the magicians or the fairies wished to punish? It may be that I was a dog or a horse, or perhaps a fiery dragon or a horrid snake. I hope it was not one of these. But, whatever it was, everyone has certainly a right to his original form, and I am resolved to find out mine. I will start early tomorrow morning, and I am sorry now I have not more pockets to my old doublet, so that I might carry more bees and more honey for my journey."

He spent the rest of the day in making a hive of twigs and straw, and when he had transferred to this some honeycombs and a colony of bees which had just swarmed, he rose before sunrise the next day, put on his leather doublet, bound his new hive to his back, and set forth on his quest, the bees who were to accompany him buzzing about him like a cloud.

As the Bee-man passed through the little village the people greatly wondered at his queer appearance, with the hive upon his back. "The Bee-man is going on a long expedition this time," they said. But no one imagined the strange business on which he was bent. About noon he sat

down under a tree, near a beautiful meadow covered with blossoms, and ate a little honey. Then he untied his hive and stretched himself out on the grass to rest. As he gazed upon his bees hovering above him, some going out to the blossoms in the sunshine, and some returning laden with the sweet pollen, he said to himself: "They know just what they have to do, and they do it. But alas for me! I know not what I may have to do. And yet, whatever it may be, I am determined to do it. In some way or other I will find out what was my original form, and then I will have myself changed back to it."

And now the thought again came to him that perhaps his original form might have been something very disagreeable, or even horrid.

"But it does not matter," he said sturdily. "Whatever I was, that shall I be again. It is not right for anyone to retain a form which does not properly belong to him. I have no doubt I shall discover my original form in the same way that I find the trees in which the wild bees hive. When I first catch sight of a bee tree I am drawn toward it, I know not how. Something says to me: 'That is what you are looking for.' In the same way I believe that I shall find my original form. When I see it, I shall be drawn toward it. Something will say to me: 'That is it.' "

When the Bee-man had rested he started off again, and in about an hour he entered a fair domain. Around him were beautiful lawns, grand trees, and lovely gardens, while at a little distance stood the stately palace of the Lord of the Domain. Richly dressed people were walking about or sitting in the shade of the trees and arbors, splendidly caparisoned horses were waiting for their riders, and everywhere were seen signs of opulence and gaiety.

"I think," said the Bee-man to himself, "that I should like to stop here for a time. If it should happen that I was originally like any of these happy creatures it would please me much."

He untied his hive, and hid it behind some bushes, and taking off his old doublet, laid that beside it. It would not do to have his bees flying about him if he wished to go among the inhabitants of this fair domain.

For two days the Bee-man wandered about the palace and its

grounds, avoiding notice as much as possible, but looking at everything. He saw handsome men and lovely ladies, the finest horses, dogs and cattle that were ever known, beautiful birds in cages, and fishes in crystal globes, and it seemed to him that the best of all living things were here collected.

At the close of the second day the Bee-man said to himself: "There is one being here toward whom I feel very much drawn, and that is the Lord of the Domain. I cannot feel certain that I was once like him, but it would be a very fine thing if it were so; and it seems impossible for me to be drawn toward any other being in the domain when I look upon him, so handsome, rich, and powerful. But I must observe him more closely, and feel more sure of the matter before applying to the sorcerers to change me back into a lord of a fair domain."

The next morning the Bee-man saw the Lord of the Domain walking in his gardens. He slipped along the shady paths, and followed him so as to observe him closely, and find out if he were really drawn toward this noble and handsome being. The Lord of the Domain walked on for some time, not noticing that the Bee-man was behind him. But suddenly turning, he saw the little old man.

"What are you doing here, you vile beggar?" he cried, and he gave him a kick that sent him into some bushes that grew by the side of the path.

The Bee-man scrambled to his feet, and ran as fast as he could to the place where he had hidden his hive and his old doublet.

"If I am certain of anything," he thought, "it is that I was never a person who would kick a poor old man. I shall leave this place. I was transformed from nothing that I see here."

He now traveled for a day or two longer, and then he came to a great black mountain, near the bottom of which was an opening like the mouth of a cave.

This mountain, he had heard, was filled with caverns and underground passages, which were the abodes of dragons, evil spirits, and horrid creatures of all kinds.

"Ah me!" said the Bee-man, with a sigh, "I suppose I ought to visit this place. If I am going to do this thing properly, I should look on all sides of the subject, and I may have been one of those dreadful creatures myself."

Thereupon he went to the mountain, and as he approached the opening of the passage which led into its inmost recesses, he saw, sitting upon the ground, and leaning his back against a tree, a Languid Youth.

"Good day," said this individual, when he saw the Bee-man. "Are you going inside?"

"Yes," said the Bee-man, "that is what I intend to do."

"Then," said the Languid Youth, slowly rising to his feet, "I think I will go with you. I was told that if I went in there I should get my energies toned up, and they need it very much. But I did not feel equal to entering by myself, and I thought I would wait until someone came who was going in. I am very glad to see you, and we will enter together."

So the two went into the cave, and they had proceeded but a short distance when they met a very little creature, whom it was easy to recognize as a Very Imp. He was about two feet high, and resembled in color a freshly polished pair of boots. He was extremely lively and active, and came bounding toward them.

"What did you two people come here for?" he asked.

"I came," said the Languid Youth, "to have my energies toned up."

"You have come to the right place," said the Very Imp. "We will tone you up. And what does that old Bee-man want?"

"He has been transformed from something, and wants to find out what it is. He thinks he may have been one of the things in here."

"I should not wonder if that were so," said the Very Imp, rolling his head on one side and eyeing the Bee-man with a critical gaze. "All right," continued the Very Imp, "he can go around and pick out his previous existence. We have here all sorts of vile creepers, crawlers, hissers, and snorters. I suppose he thinks anything will be better than a Bee-man."

"It is not because I want to be better than I am," said the Bee-man, "that I started out on this search. I have simply an honest desire to become what I originally was."

"Oh! That is it, is it?" said the other. "There is an idiotic moon-calf here, with a clam head, which must be very much like what you used to be."

"Nonsense," said the Bee-man. "You have not the least idea what an honest purpose is. I shall go about and see for myself."

"Go on," said the Very Imp, "and I will attend to this fellow who wants to be toned up." So saying, he joined the Languid Youth.

"Look here," said that individual, regarding him with interest, "do you black and shine yourself every morning?"

"No," said the other, "it is waterproof varnish. You want to be invigorated, don't you? Well, I will tell you a splendid way to begin. You see that Bee-man has put down his hive and his coat with the bees in it. Just wait till he gets out of sight, and then catch a lot of those bees and squeeze them flat. If you spread them on a sticky rag, and make a plaster, and put it on the small of your back, it will invigorate you like everything, especially if some of the bees are not quite dead."

"Yes," said the Languid Youth, looking at him with his mild eyes, "but if I had energy enough to catch a bee I would be satisfied. Suppose you catch a lot for me."

"The subject is changed," said the Very Imp. "We are now about to visit the spacious chamber of the King of the Snapdragons."

"That is a flower," said the Languid Youth.

"You will find him a gay old blossom," said the other. "When he has chased you round his room, and has blown sparks at you, and has snorted and howled, and cracked his tail, and snapped his jaws like a pair of anvils, your energies will be toned up higher than ever before in your life."

"No doubt of it," said the Languid Youth. "But I think I will begin with something a little milder."

"Well, then," said the other, "there is a flat-tailed Demon of the Gorge in here. He is generally asleep, and, if you say so, you can slip into the farthest corner of his cave, and I'll solder his tail to the opposite wall. Then he will rage and roar, but he can't get at you, for he doesn't reach all the way across his cave; I have measured him. It will tone you up wonderfully to sit there and watch him."

"Very likely," said the Languid Youth. "But I would rather stay outside and let you go up in the corner. The performance in that way will be more interesting to me."

"You are dreadfully hard to please," said the Very Imp. "I have offered them to you loose, and I have offered them fastened to a wall, and now the best thing I can do is to give you a chance at one of them that can't move at all. It is the Ghastly Griffin, and is enchanted. He can't stir so much as the tip of his whiskers for a thousand years. You can go to his cave and examine him just as if he were stuffed, and then you can sit on his back and think how it would be if you should live to be a thousand years old, and he should wake up while you are sitting there. It would be easy to imagine a lot of horrible things he would do to you when you look at his open mouth with its awful fangs, his dreadful claws, and his horrible wings all covered with spikes."

"I think that might suit me," said the Languid Youth. "I would much rather imagine the exercises of these monsters than to see them really going on."

"Come on, then," said the Very Imp, and he led the way to the cave of the Ghastly Griffin.

The Bee-man went by himself through a great part of the mountain, and looked into many of its gloomy caves and recesses, recoiling in horror from most of the dreadful monsters who met his eyes. While he was wandering about, an awful roar was heard resounding through the passages of the mountain, and soon there came flapping along an enormous dragon, with body black as night, and wings and tail of fiery red. In his great fore-claws he bore a little baby.

"Horrible!" exclaimed the Bee-man. "He is taking that little creature to some place to devour it."

He saw the dragon enter a cave not far away, and following, looked in. The dragon was crouched upon the ground, with the little baby lying before him. It did not seem to be hurt, but was frightened and crying. The monster was looking upon it with delight, as if he intended to make a dainty meal of it as soon as his appetite should be a little stronger.

"It is too bad!" thought the Bee-man. "Somebody ought to do something." And turning around, he ran away as fast as he could.

He ran through various passages until he came to the spot where he had left his beehive. Picking it up, he hurried back, carrying the hive in his two hands before him. When he reached the cave of the dragon, he looked in and saw the monster still crouched over the weeping child. Without a moment's hesitation, the Bee-man rushed into the cave and threw his hive straight into the face of the dragon. The bees, enraged by the shock, rushed out in an angry crowd, and immediately fell upon the head, mouth, eyes, and nose of the dragon. The great monster, astounded by this sudden attack, and driven almost wild by the numberless stings of the bees, sprang back to the farthest portion of his cave, still followed by his relentless enemies, at whom he flapped wildly with his great wings and struck with his paws. While the dragon was thus engaged with the bees, the Bee-man rushed forward, seized the child, and hurried away. He did not stop to pick up his doublet, but kept on until he reached the entrance of the caves. There he saw the Very Imp hopping along on one leg, and rubbing his back and shoulders with his

hands; he stopped to enquire what was the matter, and what had become of the Languid Youth.

"He is no kind of a fellow," said the Very Imp. "He disappointed me dreadfully. I took him up to the Ghastly Griffin, and told him the thing was enchanted, and that he might sit on its back and think about what it could do if it were awake. But when he came near it the wretched creature opened its eyes and raised its head, and then you ought to have seen how mad that simpleton was. He made a dash at me and seized me by the ears. He kicked and beat me till I can scarcely move."

"His energies must have been toned up a good deal," said the Bee-man.

"Toned up! I should say so!" cried the other. "I raised a howl, and a Scissor-jawed Clipper came out of his hole, and got after him. But that lazy fool ran so fast he could not be caught."

The Bee-man now ran on, and soon overtook the Languid Youth.

"You need not be in a hurry now," said the latter, "for the rules of this institution don't allow the creatures inside to come out of this opening, or to hang around it. If they did, they would frighten away visitors. They go in and out of holes in the upper part of the mountain."

The two proceeded on their way.

"What are you going to do with that baby?" said the Languid Youth.

"I shall carry it along with me as I go on with my search," said the Bee-man, "and perhaps I may find its mother. If I do not, I shall give it to somebody in the little village yonder. Anything would be better than leaving it to be devoured by that horrid dragon."

"Let me carry it. I feel quite strong enough now to carry a baby."

"Thank you," said the Bee-man, "but I can take it myself. I like to carry something, and I have now neither my hive nor my doublet."

"It is very well that you had to leave them behind," said the Youth, "for the bees would have stung the baby."

"My bees never sting babies," said the other.

"They probably never had a chance," remarked his companion.

They soon entered the village, and after walking a short distance the

Youth exclaimed: "Do you see that woman over there, sitting at the door of her house? She has beautiful hair, and she is tearing it all to pieces. She should not be allowed to do that."

"No," said the Bee-man. "Her friends should tie her hands."

"Perhaps she is the mother of this child," said the Youth, "and if you give it to her she will no longer think of tearing her hair."

"But," said the Bee-man, "you don't really think this is her child?"

"Suppose you go over and see," said the other.

The Bee-man hesitated a moment, and then he walked toward the woman. Hearing him coming, she raised her head, and when she saw the child she rushed toward it, snatched it into her arms, and screaming with joy, she covered it with kisses. Then with happy tears she begged to know the story of the rescue of her child, whom she never expected to see again. She loaded the Bee-man with thanks and blessings; the friends and neighbors gathered around and there was great rejoicing. The mother urged the Bee-man and the Youth to stay with her and rest and refresh themselves, which they were glad to do, as they were tired and hungry.

They remained at the cottage all night, and in the afternoon of the

next day the Bee-man said to the Youth: "It may seem an odd thing to you, but never in all my life have I felt myself drawn toward any living being as I am drawn toward this baby. Therefore I believe that I have been transformed from a baby."

"Good!" cried the Youth. "It is my opinion that you have hit the truth. And would you really like to be changed back to your original form?"

"Indeed I would!" said the Bee-man. "I have the strongest yearning to be what I originally was."

The Youth, who had now lost every trace of languid feeling, took a great interest in the matter, and early the next morning started off to inform the Junior Sorcerer that the Bee-man had discovered what he had been transformed from, and desired to be changed back to it.

The Junior Sorcerer and his learned masters were filled with enthusiasm when they heard this report, and they at once set out for the mother's cottage, where, by magic arts, the Bee-man was changed back into a baby. The mother was so grateful for what the Bee-man had done for her that she agreed to take charge of this baby and to bring it up with her own.

"It will be a grand thing for him," said the Junior Sorcerer, "and I am glad I studied his case. He will now have a fresh start in life, and will have a chance to become something better than a miserable old man living in a wretched hut, with no friends or companions but buzzing bees."

The Junior Sorcerer and his masters then returned to their homes, happy in the success of their great performance. And the Youth went back to his home anxious to begin a life of activity and energy.

Years and years afterward, when the Junior Sorcerer had become a Senior and was very old indeed, he passed through the country of Orn, and noticed a small hut about which swarms of bees were flying. He approached it, and looking in at the door, he saw an old man in a leather doublet, sitting at a table, eating honey. By his magic art he knew this was the baby which had been transformed from the Bee-man.

"Upon my word!" exclaimed the Sorcerer, "he has grown into the same thing again!"

THE APPLE OF CONTENTMENT

HOWARD PYLE

❖ *Howard Pyle (1853–1911) was born in Wilmington, Delaware. Pyle was an illustrator as well as an author, and his books are beautiful examples of integrated text and pictures. His artistic pupils included Maxfield Parrish and N. C. Wyeth. He is today best remembered for his artistic influence, and for his retellings of the legends of King Arthur and Robin Hood, but the prose style of these books is cumbersome and archaic. His fairy tales, collected in* **Pepper and Salt, or Seasoning for Young Folk** *(1885),* **The Wonder Clock, or Four and Twenty Marvellous Tales** *(1887), and* **Twilight Land** *(1895), together with a fantasy novel,* **The Garden Behind the Moon** *(1895), are a more enduring achievement. Although they depend heavily on the European folktale for their structure and atmosphere, an American cheerfulness and optimism has replaced the Germanic gloom; Pyle's childhood reading had, after all, included Hawthorne's* **A Wonder Book** *and* **Tanglewood Tales** *alongside the Brothers Grimm. "The Apple of Contentment" comes from* **Pepper and Salt,** *having previously appeared in the journal* **Harper's Young People;** *Pyle was also a frequent contributor to* **St. Nicholas.** *His sister Katharine Pyle (1863–1938) was also a notable children's author.* ❖

THERE WAS a woman once, and she had three daughters. The first daughter squinted with both eyes, yet the woman loved her as she loved salt, for she herself squinted with both eyes. The second daughter had one shoulder higher than the other, and eyebrows as black as soot in the

chimney, yet the woman loved her as well as she loved the other, for she herself had black eyebrows and one shoulder higher than the other. The youngest daughter was as pretty as a ripe apple, and had hair as fine as silk and the color of pure gold, but the woman loved her not at all, for, as I have said, she herself was neither pretty, nor had she hair of the color of pure gold. Why all this was so, even Hans Pfifendrummel cannot tell, though he has read many books and one over.

The first sister and the second sister dressed in their Sunday clothes every day, and sat in the sun doing nothing, just as though they had been born ladies, both of them.

As for Christine — that was the name of the youngest girl — as for Christine, she dressed in nothing but rags, and had to drive the geese to the hills in the morning and home again in the evening, so that they might feed on the young grass all day and grow fat.

The first sister and the second sister had white bread (and butter beside) and as much fresh milk as they could drink; but Christine had to eat cheese-parings and bread-crusts, and had hardly enough of them to keep Goodman Hunger from whispering in her ear.

This was how the churn clacked in that house!

Well, one morning Christine started off to the hills with her flock of geese, and in her hands she carried her knitting, at which she worked to save time. So she went along the dusty road, until, by-and-by, she came to a place where a bridge crossed the brook, and what should she see there but a little red cap, with a silver bell at the point of it, hanging from the alder branch. It was such a nice, pretty little red cap that Christine thought that she would take it home with her, for she had never seen the like of it in all of her life before.

So she put it in her pocket, and then off she went with her geese again. But she had hardly gone two-score of paces when she heard a voice calling her, "Christine! Christine!"

She looked, and who should she see but a queer little gray man, with a great head as big as a cabbage and little legs as thin as young radishes.

"What do you want?" said Christine, when the little man had come to where she was.

Oh, the little man only wanted his cap again, for without it he could not go back home into the hill — that was where he belonged.

But how did the cap come to be hanging from the bush? Yes, Christine would like to know that before she gave it back again.

Well, the little hill-man was fishing by the brook over yonder when a puff of wind blew his cap into the water, and he just hung it up to dry. That was all that there was about it; and now would Christine please give it to him?

Christine did not know how about that; perhaps she would and perhaps she would not. It was a nice, pretty little cap; what would the little underground man give her for it? That was the question.

Oh, the little man would give her five thalers for it, and gladly.

No; five thalers was not enough for such a pretty little cap — see, there was a silver bell hanging to it too.

Well, the little man did not want to be hard at a bargain; he would give her a hundred thalers for it.

No; Christine did not care for money. What else would he give for this nice, dear little cap?

"See, Christine," said the little man, "I will give you this for the cap"; and he showed her something in his hand that looked just like a bean, only it was as black as a lump of coal.

"Yes, good; but what is that?" said Christine.

"That," said the little man, "is a seed from the apple of contentment. Plant it, and from it will grow a tree, and from the tree an apple. Everybody in the world that sees the apple will long for it, but nobody in the world can pluck it but you. It will always be meat and drink to you when you are hungry, and warm clothes to your back when you are cold. Moreover, as soon as you pluck it from the tree, another as good will grow in its place. *Now*, will you give me my hat?"

Oh yes; Christine would give the little man his cap for such a seed as that, and gladly enough. So the little man gave Christine the seed, and Christine gave the little man his cap again. He put the cap on his head, and — puff! — away he was gone, as suddenly as the light of a candle when you blow it out.

So Christine took the seed home with her, and planted it before the window of her room. The next morning when she looked out of the window she beheld a beautiful tree, and on the tree hung an apple that shone in the sun as though it were pure gold. Then she went to the tree and plucked the apple as easily as though it were a gooseberry, and as soon as she had plucked it another as good grew in its place. Being hungry she ate it, and thought that she had never eaten anything as good, for it tasted like pancake with honey and milk.

By-and-by the oldest sister came out of the house and looked around, but when she saw the beautiful tree with the golden apple hanging from it you can guess how she stared.

Presently she began to long and long for the apple as she had never longed for anything in her life. "I will just pluck it," said she, "and no one will be the wiser for it." But that was easier said than done. She reached and reached, but she might as well have reached for the moon; she climbed and climbed, but she might as well have climbed for the sun — for either one would have been as easy to get as that which she wanted. At last she had to give up trying for it, and her temper was none the sweeter for that, you may be sure.

After a while came the second sister, and when she saw the golden

apple she wanted it just as much as the first had done. But to want and to get are very different things, as she soon found, for she was no more able to get it than the other had been.

Last of all came the mother, and she also strove to pluck the apple. But it was no use. She had no more luck of her trying than her daughters; all that the three could do was to stand under the tree and look at the apple, and wish for it and wish for it.

They are not the only ones who have done the like, with the apple of contentment hanging just above them.

As for Christine, she had nothing to do but to pluck an apple whenever she wanted it. Was she hungry? There was the apple hanging in the tree for her. Was she thirsty? There was the apple. Cold? There was the apple. So you see she was the happiest girl betwixt all the seven hills that stand at the ends of the earth; for nobody in the world can have more than contentment and that was what the apple brought her.

One day a king came riding along the road, and all of his people with him. He looked up and saw the apple hanging in the tree, and a great desire came upon him to have a taste of it. So he called one of the servants to him, and told him to go and ask whether it could be bought for a potful of gold.

So the servant went to the house and knocked on the door — rap! tap! tap!

"What do you want?" said the mother of the three sisters, coming to the door.

Oh, nothing much; only a king was out there in the road, and wanted to know if she would sell the apple yonder for a potful of gold.

Yes, the woman would do that. Just pay her the pot of gold and he might go and pluck it and welcome.

So the servant gave her the pot of gold, and then he tried to pluck the apple. First he reached for it, and then he climbed for it, and then he shook the limb.

But it was no use for him to try; he could no more get it — well — than I could if I had been in his place.

At last the servant had to go back to the King. The apple was there, he said, and the woman had sold it, but try and try as he would he could no more get it than he could get the little stars in the sky.

Then the King told the steward to go and get it for him; but the steward, though he was a tall man and a strong man, could no more pluck the apple than the servant.

So he had to go back to the King with an empty fist. No; he could not gather it either.

Then the King himself went. He knew that he could pluck it — of course he could! Well, he tried and tried; but nothing came of his trying,

and he had to ride away at last without having had so much as a smell of the apple.

After the King came home, he talked and dreamed and thought of nothing but the apple; for the more he could not get it the more he wanted it — that is the way we are made in this world. At last he grew melancholy and sick for want of that which he could not get. Then he sent for one who was so wise that he had more in his head than ten men together. This wise man told him that the only one who could pluck the fruit of contentment for him was the one to whom the tree belonged. This was one of the daughters of the woman who had sold the apple to him for the pot of gold.

When the King heard this he was very glad; he had his horse saddled, and he and his court rode away, and so came at last to the cottage where Christine lived. There they found the mother and the elder sisters, for Christine was away on the hills with her geese.

The King took off his hat and made a fine bow.

The wise man at home had told him this and that; now to which one of her daughters did the apple tree belong? So said the King.

"Oh, it is my oldest daughter who owns the tree," said the woman.

So, good! Then if the oldest daughter would pluck the apple for him he would take her home and marry her and make a queen of her. Only let her get it for him without delay.

Prut! That would never do. What! Was the girl to climb the apple tree before the King and all of the court! No! No! Let the King go home, and she would bring the apple to him all in good time; that was what the woman said.

Well, the King would do that, only let her make haste, for he wanted it very much indeed.

As soon as the King had gone, the woman and her daughters sent for the goose-girl to the hills. Then they told her that the King wanted the apple yonder, and that she must pluck it for her sister to take to him; if she did not do as they said they would throw her into the well. So Christine had to pluck the fruit; and as soon as she had done so the oldest sister wrapped it up in a napkin and set off with it to the King's house, as pleased as pleased could be. Rap! tap! tap! She knocked at the door. Had she brought the apple for the King?

Oh yes; she had brought it. Here it was, all wrapped up in a fine napkin.

After that they did not let her stand outside the door till her toes were cold, I can tell you. As soon as she had come to the King she opened her napkin. Believe me or not as you please, all the same, I tell you that there was nothing in the napkin but a hard round stone. When the King saw only a stone he was so angry that he stamped like a rabbit and told them to put the girl out of the house. So they did, and she went home with a flea in her ear, I can tell you.

Then the King sent his steward to the house where Christine and her sisters lived.

He told the woman that he had come to find whether she had any other daughters.

Yes; the woman had another daughter, and, to tell the truth, it was she who owned the tree. Just let the steward go home again and the girl would fetch the apple in a little while.

As soon as the steward had gone, they sent to the hills for Christine again. Look! She must pluck the apple for the second sister to take to the King; if she did not do that they would throw her into the well.

So Christine had to pluck it, and gave it to the second sister, who wrapped it up in a napkin and set off for the King's house. But she fared no better than the other, for, when she opened the napkin, there was nothing in it but a lump of mud. So they packed her home again with her apron to her eyes.

After a while the King's steward came to the house again. Had the woman no other daughter than these two?

Well, yes; there was one, but she was a poor ragged thing, of no account, and fit for nothing in the world but to tend the geese.

Where was she?

Oh, she was up on the hills now tending her flock.

But could the steward see her?

Yes, he might see her, but she was nothing but a poor simpleton.

That was all very good, but the steward would like to see her, for that was what the King had sent him there for.

So there was nothing to do but to send to the hills for Christine.

After a while she came, and the steward asked her if she could pluck the apple yonder for the King.

Yes; Christine could do that easily enough. So she reached and picked it as though it had been nothing but a gooseberry on the bush. Then the steward took off his hat and made her a low bow in spite of her ragged dress, for he saw that she was the one for whom they had been looking all this time.

So Christine slipped the golden apple into her pocket, and then she and the steward set off to the King's house together.

When they had come there everybody began to titter and laugh behind the palms of their hands to see what a poor ragged goose-girl the steward had brought home with him. But for that the steward cared not a rap.

"Have you brought the apple?" said the King, as soon as Christine had come before him.

Yes; here it was; and Christine thrust her hand into her pocket and brought it forth. Then the King took a great bite of it, and as soon as he had done so he looked at Christine and thought that he had never seen such a pretty girl. As for her rags, he minded them no more than one minds the spots on a cherry; that was because he had eaten of the apple of contentment.

And were they married? Of course they were! And a grand wedding it was, I can tell you. It is a pity that you were not there; but though you were not, Christine's mother and sisters were, and, what is more, they danced with the others, though I believe they would rather have danced upon pins and needles.

"Never mind," said they; "we still have the apple of contentment at home, though we cannot taste of it." But no; they had nothing of the kind. The next morning it stood before the young Queen Christine's window, just as it had at her old home, for it belonged to her and to no one else in all of the world. That was lucky for the King, for he needed a taste of it now and then as much as anybody else, and no one could pluck it for him but Christine.

Now that is all of this story. What does it mean? Can you not see? Prut! Rub your spectacles and look again!

ROSY'S JOURNEY

LOUISA MAY ALCOTT

➳ *Louisa May Alcott (1832–88) was born in Germantown, Pennsylvania, and described her New England childhood in the classic,* **Little Women** *(1868). The second daughter of the Utopian philosopher Amos Bronson Alcott, a friend of Ralph Waldo Emerson, she began to write as a teenager. Her earliest stories were moralistic fairy tales, published as* **Flower Fables** *(1855), but she soon moved on, like Jo March in* **Little Women**, *to lurid melodramas, only recently rediscovered and published as* **Behind a Mask** *(1975), and* **Plots and Counterplots** *(1976). In 1867 she was appointed editor of the Boston children's magazine,* **Merry's Museum**, *and also started work on* **Little Women**, *based on the "queer plays and experiences" of her childhood — though she herself would have preferred to write "a fairy book." Her fame rests on* **Little Women** *and its successors, which transformed the American family novel, but the hankering after fairy tales persisted, and many can be found scattered through the volumes of* **Aunt Jo's Scrap-Bag** *(1872–82),* **Spinning-Wheel Stories** *(1884), and* **Lulu's Library** *(1886–89). In these, though she borrowed conventions — such as the animals that Rosy helps and that give her aid in turn — from the European tradition, she created a new atmosphere of self-reliance. In "Rosy's Journey," for instance, Rosy's sturdy independence and courage lead her to a very American happy ending.* ⇜

ROSY WAS a nice little girl who lived with her mother in a small house in the woods. They were very poor, for the father had gone away to dig gold, and did not come back; so they had to work hard to get food to eat and clothes to wear. The mother spun yarn when she was able, for she was often sick, and Rosy did all she could to help. She milked the red cow and fed the hens; dug the garden, and went to town to sell the yarn and the eggs.

She was very good and sweet, and everyone loved her; but the neighbors were all poor, and could do little to help the child. So, when at last the mother died, the cow and hens and house had to be sold to pay the doctor and the debts. Then Rosy was left all alone, with no mother, no home, and no money to buy clothes and dinners with.

"What will you do?" said the people, who were very sorry for her.

"I will go and find my father," answered Rosy, bravely.

"But he is far away, and you don't know just where he is, up among the mountains. Stay with us and spin on your little wheel, and we will buy the yarn, and take care of you, dear little girl," said the kind people.

"No, I must go; for mother told me to, and my father will be glad to have me. I'm not afraid, for everyone is good to me," said Rosy, gratefully.

Then the people gave her a warm red cloak, and a basket with a little loaf and bottle of milk in it, and some pennies to buy more to eat when the bread was gone. They all kissed her, and wished her good luck; and she trotted away through the wood to find her father.

For some days she got on very well; for the wood-cutters were kind, and let her sleep in their huts, and gave her things to eat. But by and by she came to lonely places where there were no houses; and then she was afraid, and used to climb up in the trees to sleep, and had to eat berries and leaves, like the Children in the Wood.

She made a fire at night, so wild beasts would not come near her; and if she met other travelers, she was so young and innocent no one had the heart to hurt her. She was kind to everything she met; so all little creatures were friends to her, as we shall see.

One day, as she was resting by a river, she saw a tiny fish on the bank, nearly dead for want of water.

"Poor thing! Go and be happy again," she said, softly taking him up, and dropping him into the nice cool river.

"Thank you, dear child; I'll not forget, but will help you some day," said the fish, when he had taken a good drink, and felt better.

"Why, how can a tiny fish help such a great girl as I am?" laughed Rosy.

"Wait and see," answered the fish, as he swam away with a flap of his little tail.

Rosy went on her way, and forgot all about it. But she never forgot to be kind; and soon after, as she was looking in the grass for strawberries, she found a field-mouse with a broken leg.

"Help me to my nest, or my babies will starve," cried the poor thing.

"Yes, I will; and bring these berries so that you can keep still till your leg is better, and have something to eat."

Rosy took the mouse carefully in her little hand, and tied up the broken leg with a leaf of spearmint and a blade of grass. Then she carried her to the nest under the roots of an old tree, where four baby mice were squeaking sadly for their mother. She made a bed of thistledown for the sick mouse, and put close within reach all the berries and seeds she could find, and brought an acorn-cup of water from the spring, so they could be comfortable.

"Good little Rosy, I shall pay you for all this kindness some day," said the mouse, when she was done.

"I'm afraid you are not big enough to do much," answered Rosy, as she ran off to go on her journey.

"Wait and see," called the mouse; and all the little ones squeaked as if they said the same.

Some time after, as Rosy lay up in a tree, waiting for the sun to rise, she heard a great buzzing close by, and saw a fly caught in a cobweb that went from one twig to another. The big spider was trying to spin him all up, and the poor fly was struggling to get away before his legs and wings were helpless.

Rosy put up her finger and pulled down the web, and the spider ran away at once to hide under the leaves. But the happy fly sat on Rosy's hand, cleaning his wings, and buzzing so loud for joy that it sounded like a little trumpet.

"You've saved my life, and I'll save yours, if I can," said the fly, twinkling his bright eye at Rosy.

"You silly thing, you can't help me," answered Rosy, climbing down, while the fly buzzed away, saying, like the mouse and the fish, "Wait and see; wait and see."

Rosy trudged on and on, till at last she came to the sea. The mountains were on the other side; but how should she get over the wide water? No ships were there, and she had no money to hire one if there had been any; so she sat on the shore, very tired and sad, and cried a few big tears as salty as the sea.

"Hullo!" called a bubbly sort of voice close by; and the fish popped up his head.

Rosy ran to see what he wanted.

"I've come to help you over the water," said the fish.

"How can you, when I want a ship, and someone to show me the way?" answered Rosy.

"I shall just call my friend the whale, and he will take you over better than a ship, because he won't get wrecked. Don't mind if he spouts and flounces about a good deal, he is only playing; so you needn't be frightened."

95

Down dived the little fish, and Rosy waited to see what would happen; for she didn't believe such a tiny thing could really bring a whale to help her.

Presently what looked like a small island came floating through the sea; and turning round, so that its tail touched the shore, the whale said, in a roaring voice that made her jump, "Come aboard, little girl, and hold on tight, I'll carry you wherever you like."

It was rather a slippery bridge, and Rosy was rather scared at this big, strange boat; but she got safely over, and held on fast; then, with a roll and a plunge, off went the whale, spouting two fountains, while his tail steered him like the rudder of a ship.

Rosy liked it, and looked down into the deep sea, where all sorts of queer and lovely things were to be seen. Great fishes came and looked at her; dolphins played near to amuse her; the pretty nautilus sailed by in its transparent boat; and porpoises made her laugh with their rough play. Mermaids brought her pearls and red coral to wear, sea-apples to eat, and at night sung her to sleep with their sweet lullabies.

So she had a very pleasant voyage, and ran on shore with many thanks to the good whale, who gave a splendid spout, and swam away.

Then Rosy traveled along till she came to a desert. Hundreds of miles of hot sand, with no trees or brooks or houses.

"I never can go that way," she said; "I should starve, and soon be worn out walking in that hot sand. What *shall* I do?"

> "Quee, quee!
> Wait and see:
> You were good to me;
> So here I come,
> From my little home,
> To help you willingly,"

said a friendly voice; and there was the mouse, looking at her with its bright eyes full of gratitude.

"Why, you dear little thing, I'm very glad to see you; but I'm sure you can't help me across this desert," said Rosy, stroking its soft back.

"That's easy enough," answered the mouse, rubbing its paws briskly. "I'll just call my friend the lion; he lives here, and he'll take you across with pleasure."

"Oh, I'm afraid he'd rather eat me. How dare you call that fierce beast?" cried Rosy, much surprised.

"I gnawed him out of a net once, and he promised to help me. He is a noble animal, and he will keep his word."

Then the mouse sang, in its shrill little voice,

> "O lion, grand,
> Come over the sand,
> And help me now, I pray!
> Here's a little lass,
> Who wants to pass;
> Please carry her on her way."

In a moment a loud roar was heard, and a splendid yellow lion, with fiery eyes and a long mane, came bounding over the sand to meet them.

"What can I do for you, tiny friend?" he said, looking at the mouse, who was not a bit frightened, though Rosy hid behind a rock, expecting every moment to be eaten.

Mousie told him, and the good lion said pleasantly, — "I'll take the child along. Come on, my dear; sit on my back and hold fast to my mane, for I'm a swift horse, and you might fall off."

Then he crouched down like a great cat, and Rosy climbed up, for he was so kind she could not fear him; and away they went, racing over the sand till her hair whistled in the wind. As soon as she got her breath, she thought it great fun to go flying along, while other lions and tigers rolled their fierce eyes at her, but dared not touch her; for this lion was king of all, and she was quite safe. They met a train of camels with loads on their backs; and the people traveling with them wondered what queer thing was riding that fine lion. It looked like a very large monkey in a red cloak, but went so fast they never saw that it was a little girl.

"How glad I am that I was kind to the mouse; for if the good little creature had not helped me, I never could have crossed this desert," said Rosy, as the lion walked awhile to rest himself.

"And if the mouse had not gnawed me out of the net I never should have come at her call. You see, little people can conquer big ones, and make them gentle and friendly by kindness," answered the lion.

Then away they went again, faster than ever, till they came to the green country. Rosy thanked the good beast, and he ran back; for if anyone saw him, they would try to catch him.

"Now I have only to climb up these mountains and find father," thought Rosy, as she saw the great hills before her, with many steep roads winding up to the top; and far, far away rose the smoke from the huts where the men lived and dug for gold. She started off bravely, but took the wrong road, and after climbing a long while found the path ended in rocks over which she could not go. She was very tired and hungry; for her food was gone, and there were no houses in this wild place. Night was coming on, and it was so cold she was afraid she would freeze before morning, but dared not go on lest she should fall down some steep hole and be killed. Much discouraged, she lay down on the moss and cried a little; then she tried to sleep, but something kept buzzing in her ear, and looking carefully she saw a fly prancing about on the moss, as if anxious to make her listen to his song,

"Rosy, my dear,
Don't cry — I'm here
To help you all I can.
I'm only a fly,
But you'll see that I
Will keep my word like a man."

Rosy couldn't help laughing to hear the brisk little fellow talk as if he could do great things; but she was very glad to see him and hear his cheerful song, so she held out her finger, and while he sat there told him all her troubles.

"Bless your heart! my friend the eagle will carry you right up the mountains and leave you at your father's door," cried the fly; and he was off with a flirt of his gauzy wings, for he meant what he said.

Rosy was ready for her new horse, and not at all afraid after the whale and the lion; so when a great eagle swooped down and alighted near her, she just looked at his sharp claws, big eyes, and crooked beak as coolly as if he had been a cock-robin.

He liked her courage, and said kindly in his rough voice, "Hop up, little girl, and sit among my feathers. Hold me fast round the neck, or you may grow dizzy and get a fall."

Rosy nestled down among the thick gray feathers, and put both arms round his neck; and whiz they went, up, up, up, higher and higher, till the trees looked like grass, they were so far below. At first it was very cold, and Rosy cuddled deeper into her feather bed; then, as they came nearer to the sun, it grew warm, and she peeped out to see the huts standing in a green spot on the top of the mountain.

"Here we are. You'll find all the men are down in the mine at this time. They won't come up till morning; so you will have to wait for your father. Goodbye; good luck, my dear." And the eagle soared away, higher still, to his nest among the clouds.

It was night now, but fires were burning in all the houses; so Rosy went from hut to hut trying to find her father's, that she might rest while she waited; at last in one the picture of a pretty little girl hung on the

wall, and under it was written, "My Rosy." Then she knew that this was the right place; and she ate some supper, put on more wood, and went to bed, for she wanted to be fresh when her father came in the morning.

While she slept a storm came on — thunder rolled and lightning flashed, the wind blew a gale, and rain poured — but Rosy never waked till dawn, when she heard men shouting outside, "Run, run! The river is rising! We shall all be drowned!"

Rosy ran out to see what was the matter, though the wind nearly blew her away; she found that so much rain had made the river overflow till it began to wash the banks away.

"What shall I do? What shall I do?" cried Rosy, watching the men rush about like ants, getting their bags of gold ready to carry off before the water swept them away, if it became a flood.

As if in answer to her cry, Rosy heard a voice say close by,

"Splash, dash!
Rumble and crash!
Here come the beavers gay;
See what they do,
Rosy, for you
Because you helped *me* one day."

And there in the water was the little fish swimming about, while an army of beavers began to pile up earth and stones in a high bank to keep the river back. How they worked, digging and heaping with teeth and claws, and beating the earth hard with their queer tails like shovels!

Rosy and the men watched them work, glad to be safe, while the storm cleared up; and by the time the dam was made, all danger was over. Rosy looked into the faces of the rough men, hoping her father was there, and was just going to ask about him, when a great shouting rose again, and all began to run to the pit hole, saying, "The sand has fallen in! The poor fellows will be smothered! How can we get them out? how can we get them out?"

Rosy ran too, feeling as if her heart would break; for her father was down in the mine, and would die soon if air did not come to him. The men dug as hard as they could; but it was a long job, and they feared they would not be in time.

Suddenly hundreds of moles came scampering along, and began to burrow down through the earth, making many holes for air to go in; for they know how to build galleries through the ground better than men can. Everyone was so surprised they stopped to look on; for the dirt flew like rain as the busy little fellows scratched and bored as if making an underground railway.

"What does it mean?" said the men. "They work faster than we can, and better; but who sent them? Is this strange little girl a fairy?"

Before Rosy could speak, all heard a shrill, small voice singing,

> "They come at my call;
> And though they are small,
> They'll dig the passage clear;
> I never forget;
> We'll save them yet,
> For love of Rosy dear."

Then all saw a little gray mouse sitting on a stone, waving her tail about, and pointing with her tiny paw to show the moles where to dig.

The men laughed; and Rosy was telling them who she was, when a cry came from the pit, and they saw that the way was clear so they could pull the buried men up. In a minute they got ropes, and soon had ten poor fellows safe on the ground; pale and dirty, but all alive, and all shouting as if they were crazy, "Tom's got it! Tom's got it! Hooray for Tom!"

"What is it?" cried the others; and then they saw Tom come up with the biggest lump of gold ever found in the mountains.

Everyone was glad of Tom's luck; for he was a good man, and had worked a long time, and been sick, and couldn't go back to his wife and child. When he saw Rosy, he dropped the lump, and caught her up, saying, "My little girl! She's better than a million pounds of gold."

Then Rosy was very happy, and went back to the hut, and had a lovely time telling her father all about her troubles and her travels. He cried when he heard that the poor mother was dead before she could have any of the good things the gold would buy them.

"We will go away and be happy together in the pleasantest home I can find, and never part any more, my darling," said the father, kissing Rosy as she sat on his knee with her arms round his neck.

She was just going to say something very sweet to comfort him, when a fly lit on her arm and buzzed very loud,

"Don't drive me away,
But hear what I say:
Bad men want the gold;
They will steal it tonight,
And you must take flight;
So be quiet and busy and bold."

"I was afraid someone would take my lump away. I'll pack up at once, and we will creep off while the men are busy at work; though I'm afraid we can't go fast enough to be safe, if they miss us and come after," said Tom, bundling his gold into a bag and looking very sober; for some of the miners were wild fellows, and might kill him for the sake of that great lump.

But the fly sang again,

"Slip away with me,
And you will see
What a wise little thing am I;
For the road I show
No man can know,
Since it's up in the pathless sky."

Then they followed Buzz to a quiet nook in the wood; and there were the eagle and his mate waiting to fly away with them so fast and so far that no one could follow. Rosy and the bag of gold were put on the mother eagle; Tom sat astride the king bird; and away they flew to a great city, where the little girl and her father lived happily together all their lives.

THE GLASS DOG

L. FRANK BAUM

➤ *Lyman Frank Baum (1856–1919) was born in Chittenango, New York. He had a varied career as actor, journalist, shopkeeper, and salesman before turning his hand to writing. In 1900 he published* **The Wonderful Wizard of Oz,** *and the following year a collection called* **American Fairy Tales,** *from which "The Glass Dog" is taken. This book was attempting something quite new. Baum saw no need to apologize for his American settings, but not everyone saw the point. A story such as "The Glass Dog," in which one of the characters "stopped at a drug store and put his last dime in the telephone box," seemed flat and unromantic to many readers. The most praised story in* **American Fairy Tales** *is the least American, "The Queen of Quok." But in his preface to the augmented 1908 edition, Baum insisted that "ours is the age of astonishing things." This celebration of the present, and refusal to be cowed by the past, typifies Baum's spirit. Baum's determination to construct wondrous tales out of American ingredients was influenced by his own move from the Dakota Territory to Chicago in 1893, attracted by the Chicago World's Fair. Here was a new magic of human inventiveness: the operation on a large scale of the practical imagination that inspired Baum, while trimming the window of an Indiana hardware store, to construct a tin man out of everyday items. His nephew recalled, "Mr. Baum always liked to tell wild stories, with a perfectly straight face, and earnestly, as though he really believed them himself."* ⬅

AN ACCOMPLISHED wizard once lived on the top floor of a tenement house and passed his time in thoughtful study and studious thought. What he didn't know about wizardry was hardly worth knowing, for he possessed all the books and recipes of all the wizards who had lived before him; and, moreover, he had invented several wizardments himself.

This admirable person would have been completely happy but for the numerous interruptions to his studies caused by folk who came to consult him about their troubles (in which he was not interested), and by the loud knocks of the iceman, the milkman, the baker's boy, and laundryman and the peanut woman. He never dealt with any of these people; but they rapped at his door every day to see him about this or that or to try to sell him their wares. Just when he was most deeply interested in his books or engaged in watching the bubbling of a cauldron there would come a knock at his door. And after sending the intruder away he always found he had lost his train of thought or ruined his compound.

At length these interruptions aroused his anger, and he decided he must have a dog to keep people away from his door. He didn't know where to find a dog, but in the next room lived a poor glass-blower with whom he had a slight acquaintance; so he went into the man's apartment and asked:

"Where can I find a dog?"

"What sort of a dog?" inquired the glass-blower.

"A good dog. One that will bark at people and drive them away. One that will be no trouble to keep and won't expect to be fed. One that has no fleas and is neat in his habits. One that will obey me when I speak to him. In short, a good dog," said the wizard.

"Such a dog is hard to find," returned the glass-blower, who was busy making a blue glass flower pot with a pink glass rosebush in it, having green glass leaves and yellow glass roses.

The wizard watched him thoughtfully.

"Why cannot you blow me a dog out of glass?" he asked, presently.

"I can," declared the glass-blower; "but it would not bark at people, you know."

"Oh, I'll fix that easily enough," replied the other. "If I could not make a glass dog bark I would be a mighty poor wizard."

"Very well; if you can use a glass dog I'll be pleased to blow one for you. Only, you must pay for my work."

"Certainly," agreed the wizard. "But I have none of that horrid stuff you call money. You must take some of my wares in exchange."

The glass-blower considered the matter for a moment.

"Could you give me something to cure my rheumatism?" he asked.

"Oh, yes; easily."

"Then it's a bargain. I'll start the dog at once. What color of glass shall I use?"

"Pink is a pretty color," said the wizard, "and it's unusual for a dog, isn't it?"

"Very," answered the glass-blower; "but it shall be pink."

So the wizard went back to his studies and the glass-blower began to make the dog.

Next morning he entered the wizard's room with the glass dog under his arm and set it carefully upon the table. It was a beautiful pink in color, with a fine coat of spun glass, and about its neck was twisted a blue glass ribbon. Its eyes were specks of black glass and sparkled intelligently, as do many of the glass eyes worn by men.

The wizard expressed himself pleased with the glass-blower's skill and at once handed him a small vial.

"This will cure your rheumatism," he said.

"But the vial is empty!" protested the glass-blower.

"Oh, no; there is one drop of liquid in it," was the wizard's reply.

"Will one drop cure my rheumatism?" inquired the glass-blower, in wonder.

"Most certainly. That is a marvelous remedy. The one drop contained in the vial will cure instantly any kind of disease ever known to humanity. Therefore it is especially good for rheumatism. But guard it well, for it is the only drop of its kind in the world, and I've forgotten the recipe."

"Thank you," said the glass-blower, and went back to his room.

Then the wizard cast a wizzy spell and mumbled several very learned words in the wizardese language over the glass dog. Whereupon the little animal first wagged its tail from side to side, then winked his left eye knowingly, and at last began barking in a most frightful manner — that is, when you stop to consider the noise came from a pink glass dog. There is something almost astonishing in the magic arts of wizards; unless, of course, you know how to do the things yourself, when you are not expected to be surprised at them.

The wizard was as delighted as a school teacher at the success of his spell, although he was not astonished. Immediately he placed the dog outside his door, where it would bark at anyone who dared knock and so disturb the studies of its master.

The glass-blower, on returning to his room, decided not to use the one drop of wizard cure-all just then.

"My rheumatism is better today," he reflected, "and I will be wise to save the medicine for a time when I am very ill, when it will be of more service to me."

So he placed the vial in his cupboard and went to work blowing more roses out of glass. Presently he happened to think the medicine might not keep, so he started to ask the wizard about it. But when he reached the door the glass dog barked so fiercely that he dared not knock, and returned in great haste to his own room. Indeed, the poor man was quite upset at so unfriendly a reception from the dog he had himself so carefully and skillfully made.

The next morning, as he read his newspaper, he noticed an article stating that the beautiful Miss Mydas, the richest young lady in town, was very ill, and the doctors had given up hope of her recovery.

The glass-blower, although miserably poor, hard working and homely of feature, was a man of ideas. He suddenly recollected his precious medicine, and determined to use it to better advantage than relieving his own ills. He dressed himself in his best clothes, brushed his hair and combed his whiskers, washed his hands and tied his neck-tie, blackened his shoes and sponged his vest, and then put the vial of magic cure-all in his pocket. Next he locked his door, went downstairs and walked through the streets to the grand mansion where the wealthy Miss Mydas resided.

The butler opened the door and said: "No soap, no chromos, no vegetables, no hair oil, no books, no baking powder. My young lady is dying and we're well supplied for the funeral."

The glass-blower was grieved at being taken for a peddler.

"My friend," he began, proudly; but the butler interrupted him, saying: "No tombstones, either; there's a family graveyard and the monument's built."

"The graveyard won't be needed if you will permit me to speak," said the glass-blower.

"No doctors, sir; they've given up my young lady, and she's given up the doctors," continued the butler, calmly.

"I'm no doctor," returned the glass-blower.

"Nor are the others. But what is your errand?"

"I called to cure your young lady by means of a magical compound."

"Step in, please, and take a seat in the hall. I'll speak to the house-keeper," said the butler, more politely.

So he spoke to the housekeeper and the housekeeper mentioned the matter to the steward and the steward consulted the chef and the chef kissed the lady's maid and sent her to see the stranger. Thus are the very wealthy hedged around with ceremony, even when dying.

When the lady's maid heard from the glass-blower that he had a medicine which would cure her mistress, she said: "I'm glad you came."

"But," said he, "if I restore your mistress to health she must marry me."

"I'll make inquiries and see if she's willing," answered the maid, and went at once to consult Miss Mydas.

The young lady did not hesitate an instant.

"I'd marry any old thing rather than die!" she cried. "Bring him here at once!"

So the glass-blower came, poured the magic drop into a little water, gave it to the patient, and the next minute Miss Mydas was as well as she had ever been in her life.

"Dear me!" she exclaimed; "I've an engagement at the Fritters' reception tonight. Bring my pearl-colored silk, Marie, and I will begin my toilet at once. And don't forget to cancel the order for the funeral flowers and your mourning gown."

"But, Miss Mydas," remonstrated the glass-blower, who stood by, "you promised to marry me if I cured you."

"I know," said the young lady, "but we must have time to make proper announcement in the society papers and have the wedding cards engraved. Call tomorrow and we'll talk it over."

The glass-blower had not impressed her favorably as a husband, and she was glad to find an excuse for getting rid of him for a time. And she did not want to miss the Fritters' reception.

Yet the man went home filled with joy; for he thought his stratagem had succeeded and he was about to marry a rich wife who would keep him in luxury forever afterward.

The first thing he did on reaching his room was to smash his glass-blowing tools and throw them out of the window.

He then sat down to figure out ways of spending his wife's money.

The following day he called upon Miss Mydas, who was reading a novel and eating chocolate creams as happily as if she had never been ill in her life.

"Where did you get the magic compound that cured me?" she asked.

"From a learned wizard," said he; and then, thinking it would interest her, he told how he had made the glass dog for the wizard, and how it barked and kept everybody from bothering him.

"How delightful!" she said. "I've always wanted a glass dog that could bark."

"But there is only one in the world," he answered, "and it belongs to the wizard."

"You must buy it for me," said the lady.

"The wizard cares nothing for money," replied the glass-blower.

"Then you must steal it for me," she retorted. "I can never live happily another day unless I have a glass dog that can bark."

The glass-blower was much distressed at this, but said he would see what he could do. For a man should always try to please his wife, and Miss Mydas had promised to marry him within a week.

On his way home he purchased a heavy sack, and when he passed the wizard's door and the pink glass dog ran out to bark at him he threw the sack over the dog, tied the opening with a piece of twine, and carried him away to his own room.

The next day he sent the sack by a messenger boy to Miss Mydas, with his compliments, and later in the afternoon he called upon her in person, feeling quite sure he would be received with gratitude for stealing the dog she so greatly desired.

But when he came to the door and the butler opened it, what was his amazement to see the glass dog rush out and begin barking at him furiously.

"Call off your dog," he shouted, in terror.

"I can't, sir," answered the butler. "My young lady has ordered the glass dog to bark whenever you call here. You'd better look out, sir," he added, "for if it bites you, you may have glassophobia!"

This so frightened the poor glass-blower that he went away hurriedly. But he stopped at a drug store and put his last dime in the telephone box so he could talk to Miss Mydas without being bitten by the dog.

"Give me Pelf 6742!" he called.

"Hello! What is it?" said a voice.

"I want to speak with Miss Mydas," said the glass-blower.

Presently a sweet voice said: "This is Miss Mydas. What is it?"

"Why have you treated me so cruelly and set the glass dog on me?" asked the poor fellow.

"Well, to tell the truth," said the lady, "I don't like your looks. Your cheeks are pale and baggy, your hair is coarse and long, your eyes are small and red, your hands are big and rough, and you are bow-legged."

"But I can't help my looks!" pleaded the glass-blower; "and you really promised to marry me."

"If you were better looking I'd keep my promise," she returned. "But under the circumstances you are no fit mate for me, and unless you keep away from my mansion I shall set my glass dog on you!" Then she dropped the phone and would have nothing more to say.

The miserable glass-blower went home with a heart bursting with disappointment and began tying a rope to the bedpost by which to hang himself.

Someone knocked at the door, and, upon opening it, he saw the wizard.

"I've lost my dog," he announced.

"Have you, indeed?" replied the glass-blower, tying a knot in the rope.

"Yes; someone has stolen him."

"That's too bad," declared the glass-blower, indifferently.

"You must make me another," said the wizard.

"But I cannot; I've thrown away my tools."

"Then what shall I do?" asked the wizard.

"I do not know, unless you offer a reward for the dog."

"But I have no money," said the wizard.

"Offer some of your compounds, then," suggested the glass-blower, who was making a noose in the rope for his head to go through.

"The only thing I can spare," replied the wizard, thoughtfully, "is a Beauty Powder."

"What!" cried the glass-blower, throwing down the rope, "have you really such a thing?"

"Yes, indeed. Whoever takes the powder will become the most beautiful person in the world."

"If you will offer that as a reward," said the glass-blower, eagerly, "I'll try to find the dog for you, for above everything else I long to be beautiful."

"But I warn you the beauty will only be skin deep," said the wizard.

"That's all right," replied the happy glass-blower; "when I lose my skin I shan't care to remain beautiful."

"Then tell me where to find my dog and you shall have the powder," promised the wizard.

So the glass-blower went out and pretended to search, and by-and-by he returned and said: "I've discovered the dog. You will find him in the mansion of Miss Mydas."

The wizard went at once to see if this were true, and, sure enough, the glass dog ran out and began barking at him. Then the wizard spread out his hands and chanted a magic spell which sent the dog fast asleep, then he picked him up and carried him to his own room on the top floor of the tenement house.

Afterward he carried the Beauty Powder to the glass-blower as a reward, and the fellow immediately swallowed it and became the most beautiful man in the world.

The next time he called upon Miss Mydas there was no dog to bark at him, and when the young lady saw him she fell in love with his beauty at once.

"If only you were a count or a prince," she sighed, "I'd willingly marry you."

"But I am a prince," he answered; "the Prince of Dogblowers."

"Ah!" said she; "then if you are willing to accept an allowance of four dollars a week I'll order the wedding cards engraved."

The man hesitated, but when he thought of the rope hanging from his bedpost he consented to the terms.

So they were married, and the bride was very jealous of her husband's beauty and led him a dog's life. So he managed to get into debt and made her miserable in turn.

As for the glass dog, the wizard set him barking again by means of his wizardness and put him outside his door. I suppose he is there yet, and am rather sorry, for I should like to consult the wizard about the moral to this story.

THE GOLDEN WINDOWS

LAURA E. RICHARDS

➤ *Laura Elizabeth Richards (1850–1943) was born in Boston, Massachusetts; her mother was Julia Ward Howe, author of "The Battle Hymn of the Republic." She herself began to write following the birth of her first child, contributing "jingles" to* **St. Nicholas.** *She became a prolific children's author, but is now remembered mostly for the verses collected in* **Tirra Lirra: Rhymes Old and New** *(1932), especially the cheerful nonsense of "Eletelephony."* **The Golden Windows: A Book of Fables for Young and Old** *appeared in 1903; similar collections include* **The Silver Crown** *(1906) and* **The Naughty Comet** *(1910). The phrase "for young and old" in the subtitle suggests that in stories such as "The Golden Windows" she was aiming at a more subtle, layered effect than in the simple bedtime stories for which she was renowned. Her stories share with writers such as Horace Scudder and L. Frank Baum the view that everyday reality contains the truest wonders. In America, the land of opportunity, a fairy tale hero does not so much have to make his fortune, as recognize it.* ➤

ALL DAY long the little boy worked hard, in field and barn and shed, for his people were poor farmers, and could not pay a workman; but at sunset there came an hour that was all his own, for his father had given it to him. Then the boy would go up to the top of a hill and look across at another hill that rose some miles away. On this far hill stood a house with windows of clear gold and diamonds. They shone and blazed so that it made the boy wink to look at them: but after a while the people in the house put up shutters, as it seemed, and then it looked like

any common farmhouse. The boy supposed they did this because it was supper-time; and then he would go into the house and have his supper of bread and milk, and so to bed.

One day the boy's father called him and said: "You have been a good boy, and have earned a holiday. Take this day for your own; but remember that God gave it, and try to learn some good thing."

The boy thanked his father and kissed his mother; then he put a piece of bread in his pocket, and started off to find the house with the golden windows.

It was pleasant walking His bare feet made marks in the white dust, and when he looked back, the footprints seemed to be following him, and making company for him. His shadow, too, kept beside him, and would dance or run with him as he pleased; so it was very cheerful.

By and by he felt hungry; and he sat down by a brown brook that ran through the alder hedge by the roadside, and ate his bread, and drank the clear water. Then he scattered the crumbs for the birds, as his mother had taught him to do, and went on his way.

After a long time he came to a high green hill; and when he had climbed the hill, there was the house on the top; but it seemed that the shutters were up, for he could not see the golden windows. He came up to the house, and then he could well have wept, for the windows were of clear glass, like any others, and there was no gold anywhere about them.

A woman came to the door, and looked kindly at the boy, and asked him what he wanted.

"I saw the golden windows from our hilltop," he said, "and I came to see them, but now they are only glass."

The woman shook her head and laughed.

"We are poor farming people," she said, "and are not likely to have gold about our windows; but glass is better to see through."

She bade the boy sit down on the broad stone step at the door, and brought him a cup of milk and a cake, and bade him rest; then she called her daughter, a child of his own age, and nodded kindly at the two, and went back to her work.

The little girl was barefooted like himself, and wore a brown cotton gown, but her hair was golden like the windows he had seen, and her eyes were blue like the sky at noon. She led the boy about the farm, and showed him her black calf with the white star on its forehead, and he told her about his own at home, which was red like a chestnut, with four white feet. Then when they had eaten an apple together, and so had become friends, the boy asked her about the golden windows. The little girl nodded, and said she knew all about them, only he had mistaken the house.

"You have come quite the wrong way!" she said. "Come with me, and I will show you the house with the golden windows, and then you will see for yourself."

They went to a knoll that rose behind the farmhouse, and as they went the little girl told him that the golden windows could only be seen at a certain hour, about sunset.

"Yes, I know that!" said the boy.

When they reached the top of the knoll, the girl turned and pointed; and there on a hill far away stood a house with windows of clear gold and diamond, just as he had seen them. And when they looked again, the boy saw that it was his own home.

Then he told the little girl that he must go; and he gave her his best pebble, the white one with the red band, that he had carried for a year in his pocket; and she gave him three horse-chestnuts, one red like satin, one spotted, and one white like milk. He kissed her, and promised to come again, but he did not tell her what he had learned; and so he went back down the hill, and the little girl stood in the sunset light and watched him.

The way home was long, and it was dark before the boy reached his father's house; but the lamplight and firelight shone through the windows, making them almost as bright as he had seen them from the hilltop; and when he opened the door, his mother came to kiss him, and his little sister ran to throw her arms about his neck, and his father looked up and smiled from his seat by the fire.

"Have you had a good day?" asked his mother.

Yes, the boy had had a very good day.

"And have you learned anything?" asked his father.

"Yes!" said the boy. "I have learned that our house has windows of gold and diamond."

THE PRINCESS WHO COULD NOT DANCE

RUTH PLUMLY THOMPSON

> ❧ *Ruth Plumly Thompson (1893–1976) came from Philadelphia. She would probably have made a considerable name for herself as a children's writer — building on stories such as "The Princess Who Could Not Dance," published in* St. Nicholas *in April 1916, and books such as* **The Perhappsy Chaps (1918)**, *had the death of L. Frank Baum in 1919 not created a vacuum in an Oz-hungry America. In 1921 she completed the unfinished* **The Royal Book of Oz**, *and subsequently churned out a new Oz book every year until 1939, far outstripping Baum's own output. Other additions to the Oz canon followed from the illustrator John R. Neill, Jack Snow, Rachel R. Cosgrove, Eloise Jarvis McGraw and Lauren McGraw Wagner, Baum's son Frank Joslyn Baum, and great-grandson Roger S. Baum. None of these books, created to satisfy market demand, can match the originality of Baum at his best. The easy relaxed storytelling style of "The Princess Who Could Not Dance" suggests that, left to find her own way, Ruth Plumly Thompson might have rivaled, rather than simply imitated, Baum's achievement. The story has a lovely swing to it, and while its setting is that of the traditional European fairy tale, it is no tired imitation. The story sparkles with American get-up-and-go, and its expressive, vibrant language moves one step nearer than Pyle or Baum to a truly American idiom.* ❧

OH, ONCE — oh, once, dears and ducks, there was a beautiful princess who could not dance! Think of it! All the dancing-masters in the kingdom and in all the kingdoms for miles round about could do nothing with her. They came singly and doubly and then all together, and counted one, two, — one, two, three, and twirled, and bobbed, and bowed, and stamped, and swayed in and out, and whirled round like tops; and the court musicians twanged and banged and thumped, *tum-tum, tiddy-um-tum, tum-tum, tiddy-um-tum*, till their ruffled collars wilted, and their cheeks puffed out like red balloons — but still she couldn't dance.

The king tore his hair out by the handful — he didn't have much either: and the queen wept into her flowered handkerchief, while the dancing-masters explained this and then that, but the princess sadly shook her head instead of her foot, and there was an end of it. So in all the land there could be no dancing — no court balls or frolics, nor any music even, because music made the other folks dance and the princess appear ridiculous.

And oh, my dears, that kingdom grew pokier than snuff! Faces grew long and dour, and visitors to the realm most mighty scarce. And yet this princess was really bewitchingly enchanting, her hair all tumbling golden curls, and her eyes, sweethearts, as blue as the darkest part of the sky, and her cheeks as pink as the little clouds at sunset, while her feet and hands were the tiniest ever. Oh, you would have loved her to pieces! Even her name was a dancy sort of name, for it was Dianidra.

Well, poor Dianidra grew every day more thin and sad, because all the court ladies who could dance were exceedingly unkind to her. I shouldn't be surprised if they pinched her now and then. And the king was so vexed that a real princess couldn't dance, that quite often he boxed her ears. Oh, he was a crab of a king! When Dianidra went near her mother, the queen covered her face with her handkerchief, and shrieked for her smelling-salts and moaned: "A princess who cannot dance will never marry. How disgraceful! How terrible! Unhappy me!" and a good bit more that I have not time to tell you.

So Dianidra used to wander off into the garden by herself and try to puzzle it out. She used to work it out with a paper and pencil like this: 2 steps plus 2 steps, and 1 bow plus 1 dip equals the minuet. And 4 times

3 steps plus 1 turn, and 2 swings plus 1 slide equals the court glide. Then — then, because she never could put the puzzle together, she would throw herself down on the ground and weep, until the flowers thought surely that spring had come. And, dear hearts, have you guessed why? Don't think she was bewitched. Not a bit. Let me tell you the way of it. The proud old king and the weepy old queen and the stupid old dancing-masters had been so busy telling the princess how to dance that they all completely forgot to tell her what dancing was. So Dianidra had it all mixed up with her arithmetic and spelling lessons. And of course she couldn't dance, because the wisest person in the world couldn't dance with his head.

Things grew worse and worse, and pretty bad, I can tell you. And one day, after the king had been unusually crabbish, and the queen most awfully weepish, and the court ladies outrageously crossish, Dianidra decided to run away. She waited until the gate-keeper was snoring, then she stood on her tippy-toes, turned the great golden key, and slipped out into the world. She ran and ran, down the king's highway, of course, crying all the time so hard that she couldn't see where she was going. And first thing you know, *plump-p-p! bump-p-p-p!* she had run into an old lady and tumbled her head over heels in the road.

"Sugar and molasses, my dear!" cried the old lady pleasantly, bobbing up like a top, "I was just hoping something would happen."

At this, Dianidra, who had expected nothing less than a box on the ears, stopped crying and looked at the old lady curiously. Her eyes were brown and dancy, and her cheeks, though withered and old, were red as apples. In her shabby bonnet and dress she looked younger than Dianidra herself.

"Well, well!" she chuckled, picking up her things. "Who are you, my pretty?"

"I'm Dianidra, the princess who cannot dance," the princess answered, hanging her head.

"Hoity-toity!" exclaimed the old lady. "Is that why you're crying on the king's highway?"

"Oh," sobbed Dianidra, "if I could only learn to dance!"

"Come here, child," said the old lady: and putting her head to Dianidra's heart, she listened long and knowingly.

"Yes, it's there," she muttered to herself. "It's there." All of which was very puzzling to the princess. "Now, what do you know about dancing?"

"Let me see," said Dianidra, puckering up her brow and counting on her fingers. "Two turns, plus five slides, plus six steps, plus two swings, divided by a curtsey equals — Oh, dear, what does that equal? What *does* it equal?"

At that, what do you suppose happened? The old lady burst into laughter — and I mean it, really. Her bonnet tumbled off, and she laughed and laughed, and her hair tumbled down, and she laughed and laughed; her cape flew away, and still she kept laughing: till finally, in an awful chuckle, she just *disappeared*: and out of the laughter stepped the most beautiful fairy that you can imagine — with shimmery wings and smiley eyes. Dianidra was so surprised that she laughed a little bit herself.

"That's right!" said the fairy. "Before you can learn to dance, you must learn to laugh! You must laugh with your lips, and then with your heart, and then with your feet, Dianidra, for that's what dancing is. And I'm going to send you to the most wonderful dancing-masters in the world. Walk straight ahead between these tall trees till you come to yonder gray stone, and on the other side you will see your first dancing-master.

He will tell you where to find the others. Good-bye, little princess. Before the next sunrise you will be the most beautiful dancer in all the ten kingdoms."

Then, sweethearts, the fairy kissed Dianidra and flew up, up, out of sight. And I might tell you that the fairy's name was Happiness, if you have not already guessed it.

Something about the fairy kiss kept the princess laughing softly all the way along, between the tall trees till she came to the gray stone. She peeked round it curiously, and there, sure enough, was her first dancing-master — a rippling, racing, merry little brook.

"Lean down, Dianidra," called the brook. And Dianidra, obeying, was drawn gently into its arms, and away it danced with her over the stones, singing:

> "Run, don't slip — glide, don't trip!
>   Merrily, gay, that's the way,
>   Dianidra, dancing's play."

You never could guess how pleasant it was dancing with the brook. The sunbeams came, too, and joined in. But finally the brook whispered to the princess that on the top of the next hill another dancing-master was waiting. So Dianidra sprang gaily up the bank, shaking the diamond drops of water out of her sunny locks and wringing out her dress.

And straightway she began running and gliding as easily as the brook, singing all the time the bit of a song he had taught her. When she had come to the top of the hill, there, sure enough, was her second dancing-master. 'Twas the south wind. He seized Dianidra's hands and spun her round in a hundred gay circles; and she bowed and swayed as gracefully as you have seen the flowers do when the south wind dances with them.

> "Oh, off with a rush, now sway, now stay,
>   Now bend and bow, and again away!"

whispered the south wind in her ear. And away and away they danced, and Dianidra thought she would never weary of it. Over the flower-splashed hill they swept, down and down to the edge of the sea. And there the south wind left her to learn something from this, her last dancing-master.

The sea rushed toward Dianidra with his hundred dancing waves, and, catching her up in his mighty arms, drew her out to where the swells rose and fell with majestic rhythm. The dance of the sea, dear hearts, was the most beautiful of all. First he held her curled in the hollow of a giant swell, then tossed her lightly as foam on the rising crest, where she floated gently to and fro. Now with a rush a great wave ran with her merrily up the sand, teaching her the most wonderful curtsey, the curtsey the waves have been dropping to the shore for years and hundreds of years.

After she had been dancing with the sea for a long, long time, he

brought up from his treasure-chest a wonderful coral chain, and clasped it round her neck; and he wove her a crown of seaweed and pearly sea-flowers, and, with a last caress, set her high upon the beach. So happy had Dianidra been, dancing with these wonderful dancing-masters, that she hadn't noticed that the sun had slipped down behind the hill. It was night, and the moon came up out of the sea, and smiled at the runaway princess dancing over the sands. Her satin dress was torn and dripping, but she was more beautiful now than ever before, because her eyes were laughing, her lips were laughing, her heart was laughing; but more than all else, her flying feet were laughing!

It chanced that a most royal palace stood on that beach, and the princess, running and gliding like the brook, and swaying and bending as the south wind, and curtseying and dipping like the sea, danced up to the golden gates, which were open, straight into the gaily lighted ball-room! Gorgeous princesses, and queens, and ladies of high degree were dancing with princes and kings, and gentlemen of high degree, for it was the royalest ball of the year, and from the east and west, from the north and south, from all the ten kingdoms in fact, the company had gathered.

When Dianidra swept lightly into their midst, dears and ducks, it was the most surprised company ever. The musicians all stopped thumping and banging, and, with their cheeks still puffed out and their hands upraised, stared and stared. And the gorgeous princesses, and queens, and the ladies of high degree stopped right in the midst of a wonderful figure, and, with their satin slippers daintily pointed to take the next step, stared and stared. And the princes, and kings, and the gentlemen of high degree, with their courtly backs bent for the deep bow, stopped and stared and stared; and my goody! They stared the hardest of all. But Dianidra danced merrily on.

Just about as long as you could count to twenty they all stared, then — CRASH!!!! went the music, and started up the most marvelous booming — quite like the roar of the sea — and the most royal of the princes unbent his back, and ran lightly up to Dianidra, and away they whirled down the center of the room. Then — then I am sure you

would have laughed at what happened next — because all the kings and princes and gentlemen of high degree were so anxious to dance with Dianidra that they trod upon each other's toes; and in the scramble they lost their crowns, and they shoved and pushed each other quite terribly, without ever once saying "Beg pardon," or anything like that — while the princesses, and queens, and ladies of high degree grew red and then white by turns, and stamped first one foot and then the other, and whispered behind their fans, and glared at the dancing princess through their gold lorgnettes. No wonder! Dianidra, in her torn frock and seaweed crown and coral necklace, was more beautiful than all of them together; and who, after dancing with her, cared to dance with any one of them?

So she danced with each of the royal gentlemen, but oftenest, as you are already supposing, with the most royal prince; and pretty soon they danced out into the castle gardens, and perhaps she told him all about her strange dancing-masters — but that I cannot say. They spoke so very softly that I could not possibly hear one word. But after a while the prince ordered his most royal carriage, and the fifty white horses galloped over hill and dale to the palace of Dianidra's father.

There they found the crabbish king tearing out what little hair was left him, while the queen, nearly smothered with smelling-salts, was weeping more bitterly than ever, and sobbing: "A princess who could not dance was better than no princess at all!" and a good bit more that I haven't time to tell you. But when they saw Dianidra they ceased their crabbishness and weepishness straight off, and when the prince on his bended knee asked for the hand of the princess, they were overjoyed and delighted — which is the way of kings and queens.

So Dianidra and the prince were married in a year and a day, and the wedding was the most gorgeous you could imagine. As the fairy had promised, Dianidra was the most wonderful dancer in all the ten kingdoms, for in her dancing was the ripple of the brook, the swaying of the trees and flowers in the south wind, the mystery of the sea. All through the years she and the most royal prince danced together merrily, and so lived happily ever after. That, sweethearts, was the way of it.

THE LAD AND LUCK'S HOUSE

WILL BRADLEY

➤ *Will Bradley (1868–1962) is best remembered as a typographer, designer, and illustrator; he published an autobiography,* **Will Bradley, His Chap Book** *in 1955. He made two contributions to children's literature:* **Peter Poodle, Toy Maker to the King** *(1906) and* **The Wonderbox Stories** *(1916). The first of these fairy tales set in "Noodleburg" appeared in the Christmas 1915 issue of* **St. Nicholas,** *and they continued through the following year. "The Lad and Luck's House," the fifth, was first printed in the April 1916 edition. To some extent these stories, though full of zest and charm, regress from the American boldness of Scudder, Stockton, and Baum, to the safety of a European fairy tale world full of woodcutters and millers — the kind of setting that had seemed natural in the days of Susan Coolidge's* **The New-Year's Bargain** *(1872), but that Baum had discarded without a glance behind. Yet no one could mistake Bradley's stories for the work of a European writer. Billy and Bobbs are a pair of enterprising American boys, and the lad himself is a hobo in the Carl Sandburg mold.* ⇐

HERE TODAY, and there tomorrow. That is the way it is with some folks, for no sooner do they *rap, tap, tap* at the front gate of one town, than they must be tucking their toes in the dust on the road to the next.

Yes, that is the way it is with some folks; and some there are who must always be crimping and primping and fol-de-roling. Off they go, dancing and prancing, at this ball tonight and that ball tomorrow night, and then all day long they are sleepy and cross. But none of that for me.

When night comes I like to toast my shins in a cozy corner by the fire, with the good wife a-knitting and the yellow yarn dancing over the amber needles. That's the time the fairies come. I love to watch them skipping and romping in the blaze — blue ones, red ones, green ones, and sometimes, on the rarest occasions, there comes a little one of pure gold.

And in summer — my! But that is when the fairies have the good times! Out in the garden, in the honeysuckles and the cornflowers, the delphiniums and the periwinkles, and most especially in the roses, how the fairies do skip and jump and play tag! And oh, they tell such wonderful stories and sing such wonderful songs! Sometimes the wrens and thrushes accompany them, and then there is the finest concert a body ever heard!

It takes sharp eyes to see a fairy; and when you do see one, you must never jump or make a loud noise or frown. That will scare the fairy away. Most of all, though, fairies love children, and I think it is only when old people keep a little bit of childhood in their hearts that fairies come to them. That is why I am going to try and never grow old; not old in my heart, anyway, because, you see, I want the fairies always to come to me, especially winter nights before the fire. I always have a flower or two standing around on the mantel or table to tempt them, because in all the world nothing makes a fairy as happy as do flowers.

Well, one winter afternoon, when all the family were off gadding, nothing would do but I must put on my big coat and heavy boots and tramp through the snow to Neighbor Fairborn's. I grumbled and fussed as usual, for it is never easy to get me started, and in the end, of course, I was sorry; for when we came to Neighbor Fairborn's, there was a fine fire burning on the hearth, and some tea brewing and a big comfortable chair with pillows. There, too, were Billy and Bobbs looking at wonderful pictures of ships, and trains of cars, and oceans, and bridges.

So I said, "Oho! This is just the place for me!" for I knew what was going to happen. No one else knew what was going to happen, and they kept up their jabber, jabber about all sorts of uninteresting things. But as for me, I just found a comfortable place among the cushions and pillows and kept very quiet. Pretty soon a big green flame went twisting up the chimney; then there was a big red one, and a blue one, and a purple one, and then one of golden yellow. But the yellow one was not a common, everyday flame. No, sir, the yellow flame was really a beautiful Fairy, all in a robe of golden gossamer and rich jewels. I wondered if Billy and Bobbs saw her. But just then someone said, "Hush! don't make a noise." That always distracts children, so they missed her. I was sorry, too, for the Fairy was looking right at them, and with such a serious expression that I knew there were important matters on her mind.

Well, it wasn't long before the Fairy was perched upon my shoulder and whispering in my ear; and as I listened, I was filled with such wonder that never a word did I hear of what was being said in the room, no, not one single word did I hear, save only what was whispered by the Fairy.

This is what the Fairy told me:

"The Marsh King has stolen Princess Bluebell and imprisoned her on the top of Glass Mountain."

"My! Oh my!" said I. Not out loud, because it isn't necessary to speak out loud when talking to the fairies. You just think "My! Oh my!" and the fairy hears it quite as distinctly as though it were really spoken.

"Yes," continued the Fairy. "Princess Bluebell is locked in the topmost

tower of Glass Mountain, and the Marsh King has vowed and declared she shall never be free until she consents to marry Hook Nose."

"Hook Nose?" said I. "Why, that is the Marsh King's oldest son, and the ugliest Ogre in all the four quarters of the world! Never could the Marsh King be so cruel as to compel the lovely Princess Bluebell to marry the ugly Ogre Hook Nose!"

"Yes," said the Fairy, "it is really true. A great pity it is, too, for now her mother, the Queen of the Blue Mountains, weeps day long and night long in her palace, while the King of the Blue Mountains rides at the head of twenty thousand knights in gold and silver armor to make war on the King of the Marshes."

"Twenty thousand knights in gold and silver armor!" said I. "Why, that is a marvelously big army! Surely the Marsh King cannot array a host to compare with that. Already he must have been captured and the Princess Bluebell freed."

"So I thought, too," said the Fairy; "for there are few kings that could withstand the onslaught of twenty thousand knights in gold and silver armor, especially when led by the King of the Blue Mountains. But Will-o'-the-wisp, who has just come from the marshes, tells me the Marsh King sits on his throne in the heart of the great swamps and only laughs; for you see, when the heralds blow upon their bugles, and the knights fix their lances and ride forth to the charge, why, no sooner do they

reach the low lands than the great bogs and quagmires swallow them up."

"Yes," I thought, "that must certainly be true, for the marsh lands are dotted with green, shiny bogs and shallow, muddy pools where no horse and rider could possibly travel. But," said I, "were the brave knights really and truly swallowed up?"

"Yes, at first those in the front ranks were," said the Fairy, "but Will-o'-the-wisp tells me their companions quickly rescued them, so that not a single life was lost. Only, of course, their gold and silver armor was all spoiled: at least, it had to be sent back to the Blue Mountains to be cleaned."

The situation was indeed serious, and I knew the Marsh King would not leave a stone unturned to win his way against the King of the Blue Mountains. This is why:

Twenty years ago, Hans of Noodleburg found the Hoop of Gold and released the King of the Blue Mountains from a terrible enchantment. In all that while nothing had ever been heard of the wicked Witch who wrought the enchantment. It didn't take long for me to put one and one together and make two, and two and two together and make four. Then the whole story was as clear to me as crystal. Wasn't the Marsh King a brother of the Witch? Wasn't this just the sort of trick he would be apt to play in order to have revenge? Yes, there was no doubt; the Marsh King had imprisoned Princess Bluebell and would marry her to Hook Nose just to have revenge on the King and Queen of the Blue Mountains.

Well, all of this thinking and reasoning and remembering was just the same as talking out loud to the Fairy; she listened very patiently, and knew every word that passed through my mind. No doubt she thought me very dull, and that I was losing precious moments. One can never tell what a fairy is thinking; and I suspect they often lose patience at our slow wit, though, of course, they are too polite to mention it.

"What is to be done?" said I. "Have you worked out any plan?"

Well, to make a long story short, the Fairy *had* worked out a plan, and it was neither more nor less than just this: Billy and Bobbs must mount a fine white charger and ride over hill and dale to Noodleburg, where they are to hunt about — here, there, and around the corner — for Luck's House. In Luck's House are great chests full of wonderful treasures, and tucked away on the shelves there is plenty of this, that, and the other, such as would surely be worth having by anyone who would win a princess.

Yes, that is what it had come to now. The King of the Blue Mountains had made a proclamation that he who should release the Princess would win her for his bride.

Mounting a white charger and riding to Noodleburg — surely it would take brave lads to do that, to say nothing of the bravery of entering Luck's House. Did the Fairy think Billy and Bobbs could do that?

Yes, the Fairy had no doubt at all. Listen! The Fairy had a fine plan — certainly such a plan as would have been thought of only by a fairy.

This is the plan, and it all really happened.

That night, when Billy and Bobbs were asleep, the Fairy came to them on a moonbeam; with her she had a white horse with a long curly mane and tail. Then, over hill and dale, off rode Billy and Bobbs to Noodleburg. Over hill and dale to Luck's House, where they knew just what to take and what to leave. Then, mounting their horse, over hill and dale, back home they came, long, long before the cock crowed and the sun came up over Neighbor Shultz's garage.

Now, if I were ever astride a fine white charger with my feet in the stirrups, riding clipperty-crick over hill and dale to Luck's House, I know what *I* would choose when I got there. But with children I suppose it is different; at least it was with Billy and Bobbs. What they chose, or anyway all Nurse found in their pockets in the morning, was just one round pebble, one black feather from a bird's wing, one piece of string, and one chip of wood, all of which she promptly threw out of the window.

Lucky it was, I can tell you, that a little bird saw where Nurse threw these treasures; and lucky too, that the little bird told the Fairy, or else the Princess Bluebell never would — but wait! We are getting on too far in the story.

When the King of the Blue Mountains made his proclamation that he who released Princess Bluebell would win her for his bride, he certainly caused a great stir, and brave knights came from every corner of the kingdom. To see them riding out of the town gates was a wonderful sight. The gay trappings and the glint of sunlight on the polished armor and swords and spears made such a brave showing that, had it not been for his terrible swamps and bogs and the protection they gave him, the Marsh King must have trembled in fear.

Now it happened that beside the town gates, at a little rickety table, there sat an old lady, and to each knight, as he passed, she cried, "Come buy my treasures!" But when the knights looked on the table, they only laughed, for the treasures were neither more nor less than a round pebble, a black feather, a piece of string, and a chip of wood. No one knew they came from Luck's House, and so no one bought.

When it was nearly evening and the last knight had ridden through the gates, there came a poor lad who had neither horse nor sword. He thought it would be fine to rescue the Princess, because she must be very much afraid away up there on the top of Glass Mountain. But as for marrying her, that would be quite another matter. Perhaps she liked somebody else, and of course she would never think of marrying such a poor lad.

Just then the lad spied the little old lady.

"Oho!" said he, "I have only a penny or two, but these odds and ends cannot be worth much, and perhaps the old lady needs the money."

When the little old lady saw the twinkle in the lad's eyes, she knew he would be her customer, and it wasn't long before she had the pennies and he had her treasures. Then off he went down the road, whistling merrily. Had he turned to look back, he might have wondered what had become of the old lady, for she was nowhere in sight. I, for one, think she was the Fairy; but I am not certain.

When it was nearly evening and the poor lad came to the edge of the

marsh lands, he saw all the knights riding hither and thither and not knowing which way to turn. As it happened at first with the King's army, so it happened now: every rider who dared to venture into the marsh lands soon found himself floundering in the mire.

"Here is a pretty pass!" thought the lad. "At this rate it will be many a day before the Princess is freed, and old Hook Nose will most likely be the bridegroom." Then, feeling the round pebble in his pocket, he took it out and shied it at the water to see it skip.

Crash! Bang!

No sooner did the pebble strike the water than every shiny, open pool became solid stone, firm as flint and as easy to ride on as the cobbles in our town. No sooner did the knights see this firm, hard road-bed than, with a glad shout, away they rode to capture the Marsh King.

No one took even a single glance at the lad, and no one offered him a ride, so off he trudged on foot.

In the heart of the marsh lands there was a great lake of seething, boiling water, on which no ship could ever sail. In the center of the lake there was a tall mountain all of glass, which no man could ever climb, and on top of the mountain was the castle in which was imprisoned Princess Bluebell. To this castle the Marsh King had fled with Hook Nose. How they ever reached it, I do not know, but there they were, safe and sound, when the knights rode up to the edge of the lake.

"My, this is a fine sight!" thought the lad, when he at last reached the lake. "But how are the knights ever going to get to the Glass Mountain across the boiling lake? And if they reach the mountain, how can they ever climb to the topmost tower? And if they cannot climb to the topmost tower, how can they rescue Princess Bluebell? And if they do not rescue Princess Bluebell, surely she must marry old Hook Nose, which would be sad indeed."

All this while the knights were riding hither and yon, waving their spears and flashing their swords, and making the bravest showing ever seen west of the sun and east of the moon.

As for Princess Bluebell, she had cried herself to sleep. No wonder was that, either, for she could hear the Marsh King and Hook Nose tramping about downstairs and making such a noise as was quite enough to frighten anyone.

Although the lad was as brave as the bravest, it would have been a wish wasted for him to want a horse and armor, but to wish for fine clothes and buckled shoes — that was only natural, so torn and tattered were his own. "Well, at least I have a plume for my cap!" said he, and into it he tucked the black feather he had bought for a penny from the old lady at the gate back yonder. Then he put the cap on his head and — *Whisk! Boom!*

Away through the air flew the lad. Over the knights and horses, over the boiling lake, over the Glass Mountain and into the window of the topmost tower he flew, right into the presence of Princess Bluebell, who opened her eyes and looked upon him in fear and wonder.

Up went the lad's hands to doff his cap, for he would have bowed politely. But his hand found only his hair, for his cap had been brushed from his head as he passed through the window.

Of course, all the knights thought it a strange sight to see the lad flying through the air. As for the Marsh King and Hook Nose, they were so frightened they knew not which way to turn; and when they saw the cap and feather come tumbling down, they tried to run, stubbed their toes, and went tumbling topsy-turvy into the boiling lake!

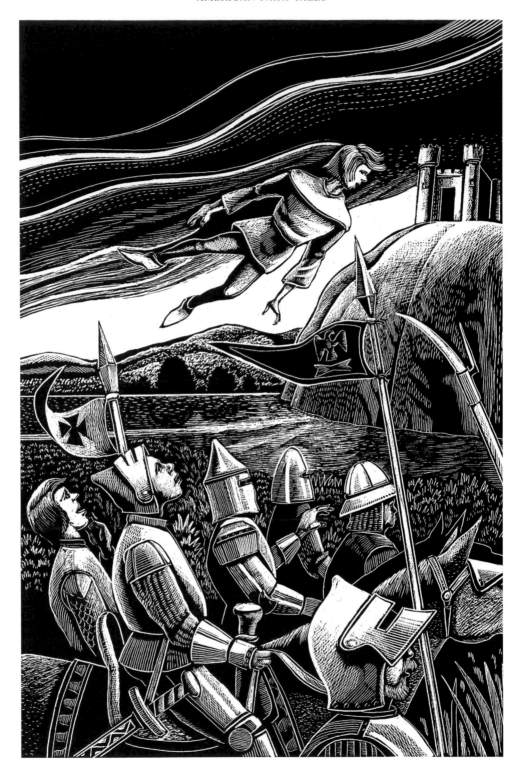

The wild shriek they gave as they reached the water made Princess Bluebell run quickly to the window. When she saw what had happened to the Marsh King and Hook Nose, and saw all the great array of knights on the opposite shore, she thought: "At last I have been rescued, and this raggedy, tattered lad must be a servant of the great prince, or king, or knight who has freed me. Now we will go home and have a fine wedding."

And then she ordered the lad to do this, that, and the other, and she smoothed her dress, and brushed her hair, and made ready to greet the fine knight whom, every second, she expected to see coming through the door.

Meanwhile, as the lad looked about and saw the high, smooth walls of the tower and the steep glass sides of the mountain and could find no way to the bottom, he thought, "This is a fine fix we are in!" A fine fix it would have been, too, if it had not been for the piece of string that came from Luck's House and was bought for a penny back yonder. Yes, the string helped them now; for no sooner did the lad lower it from a window than: *Flipperty flap!*

The finest and safest rope-ladder ever seen was hanging from the topmost tower to the very bottom of the mountain!

This way and that way swung the ladder as, step by step, down went Princess Bluebell and the lad. All the while the Princess wondered what had become of the knight, for she thought, "Surely this raggedy, tattered lad cannot be my rescuer!"

At last they reached the bottom of the ladder and the edge of the boiling lake. Now there was left only the small chip of wood — the chip brought by Billy and Bobbs from Luck's House.

Out of his pocket the lad took the chip, and into the lake he threw it. Then — *Whistle and whoop!*

Riding gracefully on the waves was — not a chip. No! The chip had become a beautiful ship with silken sails, and painted sides, and polished deck — such a ship as one might travel in all around the world and back again and never see its equal.

Well, as they sailed toward the other shore, the Princess wondered why the raggedy, tattered lad was her only companion, and, although she thought him a fine enough looking lad, she said: "Of course, he can't be the one who has freed me. My real rescuer must be one of the fine knights on the bank yonder."

Thus it was that, when the ship reached the shore, Princess Bluebell rode away with all the King's knights. Once she looked at the lad to say "Thank you," but he was coiling a rope and did not see her. So off she rode, and off rode the knights, and the lad was left behind, and —

In his pocket nothing was left from Luck's House!

The King and Queen were glad enough to have the Princess, I can tell you, and such a celebration as they made I would walk many a mile to see. Musicians played in the palace gardens. Clowns and mountebanks did tricks in the royal theatre. Ladies wore their finest gowns, and everyone had the best time ever known in the Blue Mountains.

Meanwhile, grand preparation was being made for the wedding. Artists redecorated the palace. The most famous dressmakers and milliners prepared the trousseau. The greatest chef designed and baked a wonderful wedding-cake, and no money was spared to make the event the grandest ever seen in all the world.

"But who is to be the bridegroom?" That was the question the townsfolk were asking. Every knight who had ridden into the marsh lands hoped to be the favored one, and each day so many claimed the honor that all the wise men in the kingdom could not decide which it should be.

As for Princess Bluebell, she was not at all worried. The King had said that he who freed her from the tower should win her for his bride, so of course there would be a wedding. But as the days came and went and no one proved his claim, the King finally announced a great tournament, and vowed and declared that the victor should be proclaimed the choice of the Princess.

When the King's heralds, astride their beautiful chargers and blowing great blasts upon their golden trumpets, rode to the four corners of the kingdom and cried the news of the tournament, the knights all gave a great cheer, for each one thought he surely would be the victor.

At last the great day arrived, and so many were the knights that rode to the tournament that ten men could not count them, nor twenty men their banners and the squires that attended them.

All day long the knights rode thundering forth and back across the plain with shield on arm and lance at rest, and always riders hurtled together with a splitting of shields and a splintering of lances, until so many had been tumbled from off their horses that only one remained.

I wish *I* could have been at that tournament. Some folks tell me it was the most wondrous ever seen in all the world — even surpassing any ever held by King Arthur. I wish, too, I could have seen the Green Knight when he rode thundering onto the field and challenged the victor. Where he came from, nobody seemed to know. My, how he could ride! Why, the victor, the knight who had tossed all the other knights into the dust, was tumbled out of his saddle so quickly one hadn't time to even say "*Scat.*"

Of course, there could be no doubt about it now. The Green Knight was declared the winner of the tournament, and off he rode with Princess Bluebell to the castle. All the bells in the city were ringing, and the wedding was to be held at six o'clock.

Some said the Green Knight was a great prince, and some said he was a powerful king. As for Princess Bluebell, she said nothing at all. But if you had been with her in the topmost tower of the Glass Mountain, and especially, if you had been carried down the rope-ladder and had sailed in the painted ship on the boiling lake, I think you would have taken a peek out of the corner of *your* eye, just as the Princess did. Then you would have said just as the Princess said: "Why, the Green Knight is neither more nor less than —"

Who do you think?

"THE POOR LAD!"

Yes, sure enough! The Green Knight was really the lad who had rescued the Princess. Now a raggedy, tattered lad no longer, but a rich and powerful king. All the treasures that had once belonged to the Marsh King and Hook Nose now belonged to the lad. For he was the really true and rightful king of that country.

Of course the Green Knight and Princess Bluebell were married and will live happily ever after. When they read this history, and learn of the visit to Luck's House, they will be glad Billy and Bobbs made such a wise choice. As for nurses who look through boys' pockets, and throw away stones, and strings, and other treasures, and say, "Bah! Silly truck!" — why, they had just better be careful, because I am not sure Hook Nose was drowned, and if he ever catches them and locks *them* in the topmost tower of Glass Mountain, they will be sorry they were so stupid.

HOW THEY BROKE AWAY TO GO TO THE ROOTABAGA COUNTRY

CARL SANDBURG

❧ *Carl Sandburg (1878–1967) was born in Galesburg, Illinois, of Swedish parents. He wrote an account of his childhood and youth in his classic* **Prairie-Town Boy** *(1953). Sandburg was a vigorous poet in the Walt Whitman tradition, whose* **Chicago Poems** *(1916) established him as one of the key voices of twentieth-century America. A selection for children from his* **Complete Poems** *(1970) has been published under the title* **Rainbows Are Made** *(1982). He composed the zany and exhilarating Rootabaga stories for his young daughters, "Spink," "Skabootch," and "Swipes," publishing three volumes:* **Rootabaga Stories** *(1922),* **Rootabaga Pigeons** *(1923), and* **Potato Face** *(1930). A new collection of previously unpublished tales,* **More Rootabagas***, was published in 1993. He had felt dissatisfied with the fairy tales then available, saying, "I wanted something more in the American lingo." The result was a series of stories in which the American idiom is the true hero; stories that move from phrase to phrase with intoxicated relish. This story, the first of them all, sets the tone; and it reminds us, too, of Sandburg himself, leaving home at the age of nineteen: "Now I would take to The Road. The family didn't like the idea. Papa scowled. Mama kissed me and her eyes had tears after dinner one noon when I walked out of the house with my hands free, no bag or bundle." The Rootabaga stories are, above all, fairy tales for those who walk with their hands free.* ❧

Gimme the Ax lived in a house where everything is the same as it always was.

"The chimney sits on top of the house and lets the smoke out," said Gimme the Ax. "The doorknobs open the doors. The windows are always either open or shut. We are always either upstairs or downstairs in this house. Everything is the same as it always was."

So he decided to let his children name themselves.

"The first words they speak as soon as they learn to make words shall be their names," he said. "They shall name themselves."

When the first boy came to the house of Gimme the Ax, he was named Please Gimme. When the first girl came she was named Ax Me No Questions.

And both of the children had the shadows of valleys by night in their eyes and the lights of early morning, when the sun is coming up, on their foreheads.

And the hair on top of their heads was a dark wild grass. And they loved to turn the doorknobs, open the doors, and run out to have the wind comb their hair and touch their eyes and put its six soft fingers on their foreheads.

And then because no more boys came and no more girls came, Gimme the Ax said to himself, "My first boy is my last and my last girl is my first and they picked their names themselves."

Please Gimme grew up and his ears got longer. Ax Me No Questions grew up and her ears got longer. And they kept on living in the house where everything is the same as it always was. They learned to say just as their father said, "The chimney sits on top of the house and lets the smoke out, the doorknobs open the doors, the windows are always either open or shut, we are always either upstairs or downstairs — everything is the same as it always was."

After a while they began asking each other in the cool of the evening after they had eggs for breakfast in the morning, "Who's who? How much? And what's the answer?"

"It is too much to be too long anywhere," said the tough old man,

Gimme the Ax.

And Please Gimme and Ax Me No Questions, the tough son and the tough daughter of Gimme the Ax, answered their father, "It *is* too much to be too long anywhere."

So they sold everything they had, pigs, pastures, pepper pickers, pitchforks, everything except their ragbags and a few extras.

When their neighbors saw them selling everything they had, the different neighbors said, "They are going to Kansas, to Kokomo, to Canada, to Kankakee, to Kalamazoo, to Kamchatka, to the Chattahoochee."

One little sniffer, with his eyes half shut and a mitten on his nose, laughed in his hat five ways and said, "They are going to the moon and when they get there they will find everything is the same as it always was."

All the spot cash money he got for selling everything, pigs, pastures, pepper pickers, pitchforks, Gimme the Ax put in a ragbag and slung on his back like a rag picker going home.

Then he took Please Gimme, his oldest and youngest and only son, and Ax Me No Questions, his oldest and youngest and only daughter, and went to the railroad station.

The ticket agent was sitting at the window selling railroad tickets the same as always.

"Do you wish a ticket to go away and come back or do you wish a ticket to go away and *never* come back?" the ticket agent asked wiping sleep out of his eyes.

"We wish a ticket to ride where the railroad tracks run off into the sky and never come back — send us far as the railroad rails go and then forty ways farther yet," was the reply of Gimme the Ax.

"So far? So early? So soon?" asked the ticket agent wiping more sleep out of his eyes. "Then I will give you a new ticket. It blew in. It is a long slick yellow leather slab ticket with a blue spanch across it."

Gimme the Ax thanked the ticket agent once, thanked the ticket agent twice, and then instead of thanking the ticket agent three times he opened the ragbag and took out all the spot cash money he got for selling everything, pigs, pastures, pepper pickers, pitchforks, and paid the spot cash money to the ticket agent.

Before he put it in his pocket he looked once, twice, three times at the long yellow leather slab ticket with a blue spanch across it.

Then with Please Gimme and Ax Me No Questions he got on the railroad train, showed the conductor his ticket and they started to ride to where the railroad tracks run off into the blue sky and then forty ways farther yet.

The train ran on and on. It came to the place where the railroad tracks run off into the blue sky. And it ran on and on chick chick-a-chick chick-a-chick chick-a-chick.

Sometimes the engineer hooted and tooted the whistle. Sometimes the fireman rang the bell. Sometimes the open-and-shut of the steam hog's nose choked and spit pfisty-pfoost, pfisty-pfoost, pfisty-pfoost. But no matter what happened to the whistle and the bell and the steam hog, the train ran on and on to where the railroad tracks run off into the blue sky. And then it ran on and on more and more.

Sometimes Gimme the Ax looked in his pocket, put his fingers in and took out the long slick yellow leather slab ticket with a blue spanch across it.

"Not even the Kings of Egypt with all their climbing camels, and all their speedy, spotted, lucky lizards, ever had a ride like this," he said to his children.

Then something happened. They met another train running on the same track. One train was going one way. The other was going the other way. They met. They passed each other.

"What was it — what happened?" the children asked their father.

"One train went over, the other train went under," he answered. "This is the Over and Under Country. Nobody gets out of the way of anybody else. They either go over or under."

Next they came to the country of the balloon pickers. Hanging down from the sky strung on strings so fine the eye could not see them at first, was the balloon crop of that summer. The sky was thick with balloons. Red, blue, yellow balloons; white, purple, and orange balloons — peach, watermelon, and potato balloons — rye loaf and wheat loaf balloons — link sausage and pork chop balloons — they floated and filled the sky.

The balloon pickers were walking on high stilts picking balloons. Each picker had his own stilts, long or short. For picking balloons near the ground he had short stilts. If he wanted to pick far and high he walked on a far and high pair of stilts.

Baby pickers on baby stilts were picking baby balloons. When they fell off the stilts the handful of balloons they were holding kept them in the air till they got their feet into the stilts again.

"Who is that away up there in the sky climbing like a bird in the morning?" Ax Me No Questions asked her father.

"He was singing too happy," replied the father. The songs came out of his neck and made him so light the balloons pulled him off his stilts."

"Will he ever come down again back to his own people?"

"Yes, his heart will get heavy when his songs are all gone. Then he will drop down to his stilts again."

The train was running on and on. The engineer hooted and tooted the whistle when he felt like it. The fireman rang the bell when he felt that way. And sometimes the open-and-shut of the steam hog had to go pfisty-pfoost, pfisty-pfoost.

"Next is the country where the circus clowns come from," said Gimme the Ax to his son and daughter. "Keep your eyes open."

They did keep their eyes open. They saw cities with ovens, long and short ovens, fat stubby ovens, lean lank ovens, all for baking either long or short clowns, or fat and stubby or lean and lank clowns.

After each clown was baked in the oven it was taken out into the sunshine and put to stand like a big white doll with a red mouth leaning against the fence.

Two men came along to each baked clown standing still like a doll. One man threw a bucket of white fire over it. The second man pumped a wind pump with a living red wind through the red mouth.

The clown rubbed his eyes, opened his mouth, twisted his neck, wiggled his ears, wriggled his toes, jumped away from the fence and began turning handsprings, cartwheels, somersaults and flipflops in the sawdust ring near the fence.

"The next we come to is the Rootabaga Country where the big city is the Village of Liver-and-Onions," said Gimme the Ax, looking again in his pocket to be sure he had the long slick yellow leather slab ticket with a blue spanch across it.

The train ran on and on till it stopped running straight and began running in zigzags like one letter Z put next to another Z and the next and the next.

The tracks and the rails and the ties and the spikes under the train all stopped being straight and changed to zigzags like one letter Z and another letter Z put next after the other.

"It seems like we go half way and then back up," said Ax Me No Questions.

"Look out of the window and see if the pigs have bibs on," said Gimme the Ax. "If the pigs are wearing bibs then this is the Rootabaga Country."

And they looked out of the zigzagging windows of the zigzagging cars and the first pigs they saw had bibs on. And the next pigs and the next pigs they saw all had bibs on.

The checker pigs had checker bibs on, the striped pigs had striped bibs on. And the polka dot pigs had polka dot bibs on.

"Who fixes it for the pigs to have bibs on?" Please Gimme asked his father.

"The fathers and mothers fix it," answered Gimme the Ax. "The checker pigs have checker fathers and mothers. The striped pigs have striped fathers and mothers. And the polka dot pigs have polka dot fathers and mothers."

And the train went zigzagging on and on running on the tracks and the rails and the spikes and the ties which were all zigzag like the letter Z and the letter Z.

And after a while the train zigzagged on into the Village of Liver-and-Onions, known as the biggest city in the big, big Rootabaga Country.

And so if you are going to the Rootabaga Country you will know when you get there because the railroad tracks change from straight to zigzag, the pigs have bibs on, and it is the fathers and mothers who fix it.

And if you start to go to that country remember first you must sell everything you have, pigs, pastures, pepper pickers, pitchforks, put the spot cash money in a ragbag and go to the railroad station and ask the ticket agent for a long slick yellow leather slab ticket with a blue spanch across it.

And you mustn't be surprised if the ticket agent wipes sleep from his eyes and asks, "So far? So early? So soon?"

AFTERWORD

"AMERICAN FAIRY TALES! There's no such thing."

That was the reaction of many of the people to whom I spoke about this anthology in its early stages. Yet, as the stories in this book show, from the very beginnings of American literature, American writers have striven to adapt the heritage of the European fairy tale to the new American context.

Writers such as Arna Wendell Bontemps, Sid Fleischman, Virginia Hamilton, Randall Jarrell, Maurice Sendak, James Thurber, Jay Williams, and Jane Yolen — to name but a few at random — have shown in more recent years how vigorously the fairy tale has developed in America. This anthology traces the first century of that progress, from Washington Irving's "Rip Van Winkle" in 1819 to Carl Sandburg's "How They Broke Away to Go to the Rootabaga Country" in 1923.

The fairy tale attracts writers for various reasons, but many prize it for the way in which it allows them to slip, as it were, *behind* reality. In the fairy tale world, where the laws of magic supersede the laws of logic, writers abandon the *real* in search of the *true*. It is a world in which our deepest fears and desires are given shape. Its characters represent not other people but our inner selves. In fairy tales, pure emotion is the most powerful force. Wishes are stronger than facts.

The fairy tale unfolds, in the happy phrase of the folklorist Joseph Jacobs, in "bright trains of images." The essence of the fairy tale is its utter faith in the transforming power of the imagination. In a fairy tale, for instance, a girl escaping from an ogre may toss behind her ordinary objects — a comb, a mirror — which turn into obstacles — a forest, a lake. The logic operating here assumes that *thought* is magically potent. The story moves like a dream from image to image, not event to event.

Like dreams, fairy tales resist explanation. The same story may be understood by different readers — or the same reader at different times — as an emotional drama, as a spiritual quest, or as a political satire. The fairy tale does not explain; it explores. As the Scottish fairy tale writer George MacDonald wrote in an essay on "The Fantastic Imagination" (1908), "It is there not so much to convey a meaning as to wake a meaning."

It is a mistake to think that such stories are just for children. To do so is to deny the imagination. As George MacDonald puts it, "He who will be a man, and will not be a child, must — he cannot help himself — become a little man."

Most fairy tales (or wonder tales as they might better be called, for many contain no fairies) belong to oral tradition. Many, such as "Cinderella," may be found in variant forms almost all over the world. Such tales are the root stock of every story ever told. They have been imported into the United States with each wave of immigrants, and many have naturalized here. This book is not directly concerned with such folk traditions, but rather with the literary fairy tale.

A literary fairy tale is an original, made-up story with a single named author and a fixed text. Of course elements of literary and oral tradition are constantly cross-fertilizing, so one can never completely separate the two. But for a quick rule of thumb it is safe to say that the Brothers Grimm — although they rewrote the tales they collected — represent the oral tradition, while Hans Christian Andersen — although he retold some stories he heard as a child — represents the literary one.

The story of the making of the American fairy tale begins with Washington Irving and Nathaniel Hawthorne. Both of these writers had the kind of maverick imaginations that are drawn to fantasy and fairy tale, and both tried in the early nineteenth century to translate European stories into American terms. In 1819 Irving relocated European legends to the Catskills (Kaatskills) in "Rip Van Winkle" and to the Hudson Valley in "The Legend of Sleepy Hollow"; Hawthorne imported the Greek myths to rural Massachusetts in *A Wonder Book* (1852) and *Tanglewood Tales* (1853).

Hawthorne expressed his dilemma in the preface to *The Marble Faun* (1860). "No author," he wrote, "without a trial, can conceive of the difficulty of writing a Romance about a country where there is no shadow of antiquity, no mystery, no picturesque and gloomy wrong, nor anything but a commonplace prosperity, in broad and simple daylight, as is happily the case with my dear native land."

The critic Selma G. Lanes makes the same point in different terms in her essay "America as Fairy Tale" (1971). In the New World, "on the whole, life promised more than any fairy tale. What happier ending could be envisioned — not to a make-believe tale, but to life itself — than that any small American boy might grow up to be President, or any young girl his wife? No glass slippers needed, thank you, and no fairy godmothers. Fairy tales were consolations for lives in need of magical solutions; but here man was master of his fate."

Lanes points out that "in most home-grown American fairy tales, no magic is ever more powerful than the overriding reality of the American life experience." Thus in "Rip Van Winkle" the true wonder is not that Rip has been kept in a magic slumber but that "a new nation has been miraculously born while he slept."

In L. Frank Baum's *Ozma of Oz* (1907), Princess Langwidere asks Dorothy, "Are you of royal blood?" Dorothy's confident reply is, "Better than that, ma'am. I come from Kansas."

Here, Baum turns on its head Hawthorne's view that America is too "commonplace" for Romance; for Dorothy, and her author, to be an American is more romantic than anything. One of the defining themes of the American fairy tale is this sense that ordinary life is something that the fairy tale hero must learn to value and enjoy, rather than something from which he must escape. As Mrs. Meadows puts it in Joel Chandler Harris's *Little Mr. Thimblefinger and His Queer Country* (1897), "a hut where happiness lives is a much finer place than the finest castle." Laura E. Richards's delicately poised "The Golden Windows" has a hero setting out in search of magic and finding the everyday; yet he is enriched, not disillusioned. The poor couple at the close of Horace Scudder's "The Rich Man's Place" would not exchange their love for wealth or power.

The balance between the romantic and the commonplace is not easily held. The pages of *St. Nicholas* are full of incongruous verses and stories in which fairies grapple with newfangled devices such as the telephone. Bennet W. Musson's "Through Fairyland in a Hansom Cab" (*St. Nicholas,* February 1902) shows the perceived clash between traditional fairyland and the modern world at its cheekiest. At the end, the fairies, coaxed out into the world, are horrified to be greeted by "the opening of the electric railway":

"Electricity!" shrieked the fairies wildly.

"There's the Modern Spirit in front!" cried the queen.

"Run! Run for your lives!" They all rushed into the cave.

Gretchen watched them until the last fairy disappeared.

For Carl Sandburg, a mere twenty years later, such a contrast between the world of the imagination and the world of "the Modern Spirit" had become meaningless; a typical Rootabaga tale is called "The Two Skyscrapers Who Decided to Have a Child." Sandburg, having ridden the boxcars as a teenage hobo, sees the railroad as a symbol of romance and adventure. For Gimme the Ax, a railroad ticket is a magic talisman, representing as it does the forward movement at the heart of American culture.

Although several writers tried to settle European-style fairies into the American landscape, by and large the American fairy tale before Baum and Sandburg was modeled on the twin inspirations of Andersen and Grimm. A quasi-European setting was regarded as the most suitable for fairy stories, and some good work was done in this mode, of which Howard Pyle's fairy tales, such as "The Apple of Contentment," were the most consistently successful. A longer tale in the same style that still reads well today is "Rumpty-Dudget's Tower," by Nathaniel Hawthorne's son Julian, first published in *St. Nicholas* in 1879, and recently reprinted in Mark I. West's pioneering anthology *Before Oz* (1989).

However, by 1916, when Will Bradley published his European-style *Wonderbox Stories*, including "The Lad and Luck's House," such storytelling was beginning to seem outmoded in the American context. Some of the problems are dramatized in Joel Chandler Harris's longwinded but amusing *Wally Wanderoon and His Story-telling Machine* (1904). The "story-telling machine" is a man in a cupboard. Wally says: "I have caught and pickled this man, as you may say, because he is one of the old-fashioned story-tellers. He's the last of his kind so far as I know, and is one of the worst."

At the end, Wally goes off in search of "the Good Old Times," adding, "and I hope to find a better story-teller than the one you have heard." And it does seem that somehow the old stories were, despite their many delights, failing American children in a deep-seated way. In 1877, Arlo Bates published a lively tale in

St. Nicholas entitled "The King and the Three Travellers." In it, a king encounters three men who offer to tell him "strange and unheard tales." He replied, "If you can tell stories worth hearing, you are indeed welcome. The court storyteller has just been banished for presuming to tell the same story twice." The repetition of old themes, even by writers as confident and inventive as Pyle or Bradley, was no longer enough.

All the writers in this book — including Pyle and Bradley — were part of the American search for "strange and unheard tales" that would ring the changes on the European fairy tale conventions. In classic fairy tales, the characters may, by means of a series of trials, earn their true happiness, or, by means of a series of transformations, discover their true selves. This holds true in America, but with a twist. For Dianidra in Ruth Plumly Thompson's "The Princess Who Could Not Dance," the enemy she must overcome is no ogre or wicked parent, but her own sober step-by-step intellect; she is already happy, but she does not know it. At the end of Frank Stockton's witty "The Bee-man of Orn," the result of magically transforming the Bee-man back into a baby is simply that "he has grown into the same thing again!" He was already himself in the first place.

Sometimes, as in Pyle or Scudder's prizing of contentment over riches, or Stockton's emphasis on the search for self-knowledge, the American writers redefined the idea of what "making good" might mean in a fairy tale. Sometimes, as in the case of M. S. B., or Ruth Plumly Thompson, they revitalized the language of storytelling with exuberant new American idioms.

It was not just theme and language, but also setting that needed to be made new. Writers such as Scudder, Stockton, and Alcott were feeling their way toward the creation of a shadow-America in which the dream-logic of the fairy tale could operate. The world of Scudder's "The Rich Man's Place," and Alcott's "Rosy's Journey," is both America and not-America. There is no attempt at realism, but — despite the camels and lions Rosy encounters — we are quite clearly in the United States. Scudder's "rich man" is a nineteenth-century robber baron industrialist, or a prototype of Citizen Kane; Rosy and her gold-rush miner father end up not in a castle or an enchanted forest, but "a great city."

Another story in Alcott's *Lulu's Library* (1886), "The Candy Country," sends a girl called Lily to Candy-land, where "A lime-drop boy and a little pink checkerberry girl were her favorite playmates; and they had fine times making mud-pies by scraping the chocolate rocks and mixing this dust with honey from the wells near by." There are hints here of the kinds of truly American fairyland that Baum and Sandburg were to create.

In 1901, Baum published a book with the same title as this one, *American Fairy Tales,* containing original stories — such as "The Glass Dog" — that, he was to claim, "bear the stamp of our own times." He unashamedly set wonder tales in the streets of Chicago, a boldly original move that did not find favor. It was, however, a logical extension of the "modernized fairy tale" he had published the previous year, *The Wonderful Wizard of Oz.*

This novel of Baum's, which spawned a long-running series, is now seen as the quintessential American fairy tale. In the land of Oz, Baum created a fairyland shaped to the imaginative needs of the American child. The novelist Frederick Buechner speaks for many when he writes in his spiritual memoir *The Sacred Journey* (1982) of the powerful hold Oz had over his imagination as a sick child in the 1930s:

> I lived, as much as I could be said to live anywhere, not in the United States of America but in the Land of Oz. One Oz book after another I read or had read to me until the world where animals can speak, and magic is common as grass, and no one dies, was so much more real to me than the world of my own room that if I had had occasion to be homesick then, it would have been Oz, not home, that I would have been homesick for as in a way I am homesick for it still.

To create an imaginary land that America's children could be homesick for: this is, as Baum himself touchingly wrote, "as great an achievement as to become President of the United States."

Baum built on foundations laid by many writers from Irving on, but in the Oz books and the neglected *American Fairy Tales* he was the first to give uninhibited expression to the forward-looking optimism of the American dream.

And if Baum was that dream's chronicler, Carl Sandburg, spinning nonsense tales of the Rootabaga Country for his daughters, was to be its poet. The moment in Sandburg's "How They Broke Away to Go to the Rootabaga Country" in which Gimme the Ax and his children sell all their belongings for "spot cash money" and buy railroad tickets "to go away and *never* come back" is the moment in which the American fairy tale finally came of age. To go away and never come back: that is a true fairy tale choice, but not one found in the European tradition. There, the traveler will eventually return home, even if, like Rip Van Winkle, he finds all changed when he gets there.

It is not just the sense of not looking back that makes the Rootabaga stories so special. Unlike Baum, whose prose style can best be described as workmanlike, Sandburg realized that true American fairy tales must be "in the American lingo." His use of American speech rhythms, and the muscular newness of his richly inventive language, make the stories sing from the page.

With Baum and Sandburg, the fairy tale in America had finally become the American fairy tale.

— Neil Philip

SOURCES AND BACKGROUND

Alcott, Louisa May *Lulu's Library*, Boston: Roberts Brothers, 1886–89.
See also Stern, Madeleine B. *Louisa May Alcott*, Norman: University of Oklahoma Press, 1950. Revised 1985. Meigs, Cornelia. *Loiusa M. Alcott and the American Family Story*. London: The Bodley Head, 1970.
M. S. B. "What They Did Not Do on the Birthday of Jacob Abbott B., Familiarly Called Snibbuggledy-boozledom." In *St. Nicholas*, Vol. 3. New York: Scribner & Co., 1876.
Baum, L. Frank. *American Fairy Tales*. Chicago: George M. Hill Company, 1901. Second edition, Indianapolis: Bobbs-Merrill, 1908.
See also Baum, Frank Joslyn and Russell P. MacFall. *To Please a Child: A Biography of L. Frank Baum*. Chicago: Reilly & Lee Co., 1961.
Bradley, Will. "The Lad and Luck's House." In *St. Nicholas*, Vol. 43. New York: Scribner & Co., 1916. Collected in *The Wonderbox Stories*. New York: The Century Co., 1916.
See also Bradley, Will. *Will Bradley, His Chap Book*. New York: The Typophiles, 1955.
Hawthorne, Nathaniel. "Feathertop" first published in the *International Monthly Magazine,* 1852, and included in *Mosses from an Old Manse*. Second edition, Boston: Ticknor & Fields, 1854.
See also McIntosh, James, ed. *Nathaniel Hawthorne's Tales*. New York and London: W. W. Norton and Company, 1987.
Irving, Washington. *The Sketch Book of Geoffrey Crayon, Gent*. New York: G. P. Putnam, 1848 (first published 1819–20).
See also Bowden, Mary Weatherspoon. *Washington Irving*. New York: Twayne, 1981.
Pyle, Howard. *Pepper and Salt, or Seasoning for Young Folk*. New York: Harper and Brothers, 1886.
See also Morse, Willard R. and Gertrude Brincklé. *Howard Pyle: A Record of His Illustrations and Writings*. Wilmington, Delaware: The Wilmington Society of the Fine Arts, 1921. Nesbitt, Elizabeth. *Howard Pyle*. London: The Bodley Head, 1968.
Richards, Laura E. *The Golden Windows: A Book of Fables for Young and Old*. Boston: Little, Brown and Company, 1903.
Sandburg, Carl. *Rootabaga Stories*. New York: Harcourt, Brace & Co., 1922.
See also Sandburg, Carl. *The Letters of Carl Sandburg*. Edited by Herbert Mitgang. New York: Harcourt, Brace & World, Inc., 1968. Lynn, Joanne. *"Hyacinths and Biscuits in the Village of Liver-and-Onions: Sandburg's Rootabaga Stories."* In *Children's Literature*, Vol. 8. New Haven and London: Yale University Press, 1980. Niven, Penelope. *Carl Sandburg: A Biography*. New York: Charles Scribner's Sons, 1991.
Scudder, Horace Elisha. *Dream Children*. Cambridge, Massachusetts: Sever & Francis, 1864.
See also Westergaard, Waldemar, ed. *The Andersen-Scudder Letters*. Berkeley and Los Angeles: University of California Press, 1949.
Stockton, Frank R. *The Bee-man of Orn and Other Fanciful Tales*. New York: Scribners, 1887.
See also Zipes, Jack, ed. *The Fairy Tales of Frank Stockton*. New York: Signet, 1990. Griffin, Martin I. J. *Frank R. Stockton: A Critical Biography*. Philadelphia: University of Philadelphia Press, 1939.
Thompson, Ruth Plumly. "The Princess Who Could Not Dance." In *St. Nicholas,* Vol. 43. New York: Scribner & Co., 1916.

FURTHER READING

Attebery, Brian. *The Fantasy Tradition in American Literature: From Irving to Le Guin.* Bloomington: Indiana University Press, 1980.

Buechner, Frederick. *The Sacred Journey.* London: Chatto & Windus, 1982.

Lanes, Selma G. "America as Fairy Tale." In *Down the Rabbit Hole: Adventures and Misadventures in the Realm of Children's Literature.* New York: Atheneum, 1971.

Lewis, C. S. "Sometimes Fairy Tales May Say Best What's to Be Said." In *On Stories.* New York: Harcourt, Brace, Jovanovich, 1982.

Lurie, Alison, ed. *The Oxford Book of Modern Fairy Tales.* Oxford and New York: Oxford University Press, 1993.

MacDonald, George. "The Fantastic Imagination." In *A Peculiar Gift: Nineteenth Century Writings on Books for Children,* edited by Lance Salway. Harmondsworth, England: Kestrel Books, 1976. Originally published in *A Dish of Orts.* London: Edwin Dalton, 1908.

Sale, Roger. *Fairy Tales and After: From Snow White to E. B. White.* Cambridge, Massachusetts and London: Harvard University Press, 1978.

Tolkien, J. R. R. "On Fairy Stories." In *Tree and Leaf.* London: George Allen & Unwin, 1964.

West, Mark I., ed. *Before Oz: Juvenile Fantasy Stories from Nineteenth-Century America.* Hamden, Connecticut: Archon Books, 1989.

Yolen, Jane. *Touch Magic: Fantasy, Faerie and Folklore in the Literature of Childhood.* New York: Philomel Books, 1981.

Zipes, Jack. *Victorian Fairy Tales: The Revolt of the Fairies and Elves.* New York and London: Methuen Inc., 1987. *Spells of Enchantment: The Wondrous Fairy Tales of Western Culture.* New York and London: Viking, 1991.

A NOTE ON THE EDITOR AND ILLUSTRATOR

NEIL PHILIP was born in York, England, in 1955. He studied English Language and Literature at Oxford University, and then earned a PhD on the use of myth and folklore in children's literature at the University of London. He has written widely both on children's books and folk and fairy tales, and his books include *The Cinderella Story* (1989), *The Penguin Book of English Folktales* (1992), and *The Penguin Book of Scottish Folktales* (1995). His critical study of the children's writer Alan Garner, *A Fine Anger* (1981), won the first Children's Literature Association Literary Criticism Book Award. He has edited collections of fairy tales by Charles Perrault, Oscar Wilde, Hans Christian Andersen, and others, and his own children's books include *The Tale of Sir Gawain* (1987), *The Arabian Nights* (1994), and *The Illustrated Book of Myths* (1995).

He determined to trace the history of the American fairy tale after first reading Carl Sandburg's *Rootabaga Stories* — American classics that are virtually unknown in Britain. This is his second collaboration with the distinguished American illustrator Michael McCurdy, following their acclaimed anthology, *Singing America: Poems That Define a Nation* (1995). He is married, and lives in the Cotswolds, England, a few miles from the village of Great Barrington, visiting the United States as often as he can. He believes, with the poet William Blake, that "This world of Imagination is the world of Eternity."

MICHAEL McCURDY was born in New York City in 1942. He graduated from the School of the Museum of Fine Arts in Boston and Tufts University, and subsequently spent time in Europe and the Soviet Union on a traveling scholarship. His vigorous scratchboard drawings and wood engravings are in an American line stretching back to wood engravers such as Lynd Ward, and graphic artists such as Will Bradley. Like Bradley, Howard Pyle (to whom he is related by marriage), and Frank Stockton (who trained as a wood engraver), McCurdy has combined illustration with writing, and his own books for children include *The Old Man and the Fiddle* (1992). He has also edited and illustrated Frederick Douglass's autobiography, *Escape from Slavery: the Boyhood of Frederick Douglass* (1994), and *The Gettysburg Address* (1995). He has illustrated many books for adults and children, including Mary Pope Osborne's *American Tall Tales* (1991), David Mamet's *Passover* (1995), and *Lucy's Christmas* (1994) and *Lucy's Summer* (1995), by the poet Donald Hall. McCurdy has had a long association with American poets and writers through his own Penmaen Press Books. He lives on an old farm in Great Barrington, Massachusetts, with his wife and two children, and is a Fellow at Simon's Rock College in Great Barrington.